CRUISING INTO DANGER

A SUNNY MEADOWS & KALLI BALLAS CROSSOVER

KARI LEE TOWNSEND

To my own partner-in-crime and cruising buddy, my husband of thirty-four-years, Brian Townsend. May our future always be bright, our adventures be full of many more years and cruises together, and our growing family be healthy and happy.

1

SUNNY

"What is that?" I shielded my eyes with my hand as I looked over the railing. The sun was shining, the smell of the sea in the air, and sounds of a busy harbor buzzed from down below.

A rush of excitement filled me.

Detective Mitch Stone and I stood on the upper deck of the cruise ship we'd booked out of New York City to Bermuda, waiting to depart. The Love Boat from that old TV show was made by the same cruise line as the boat we were on now, which I thought was so romantic. It was spring and still chilly in the city, but the islands would be in the seventies. Not too hot and not too cold.

Perfect weather for our escape from reality.

We were both originally from the Big Apple but now live in the small, quaint, upstate NY town of Divinity. After the birth of our second child, I'd finally convinced my husband of two years that we needed some time away alone together. He'd reluctantly agreed but only to a four-night, five-day cruise.

The man was super protective of me but even more so over our children.

"I don't know, Tink," he finally answered my question. "Maybe there's a festival going on."

Mitch had called me Tink—short for Tinkerbelle on account of my blond-haired, green-eyed pixie-like appearance—since we'd met, while I called him Grumpy Pants. It worked for us. He towered over me, sporting short black hair, chiseled features, and a jagged scar along his whisker covered jaw.

He squinted his stormy grey eyes to study the scene. "It looks like Mount Olympus down there."

"That's no festival," said another tall man with thick, wavy coffee-colored hair, olive skin, a heavily whiskered face, and piercing blue eyes.

"It's not?" I leaned past Mitch so I could see the man better.

I watched the woman by his side roll her green eyes, which were a shade darker than mine. She tucked her long, golden blond hair behind her ear and let out a big sigh. "Nope. That's my big, fat, Greek family."

"Gotcha," was all I could think to say, although I didn't really *get* her at all. The woman didn't look Greek to me, but what did I know? Taking in the spectacle down on the dock, my jaw unhinged.

I'd never seen anything like it.

Greek men, women, and children of all ages lined the dock, dancing, singing, and tossing back some kind of liquid while shouting what sounded like, "Opa!" There were so many of them, but a few stood out. An elderly woman with a scarf around her gray bun chased what looked like a grown woman in pigtails as she skipped along the pier. Another woman in polyester pants with the biggest beehive of teased black hair I'd ever seen was holding up colorful jewelry while shouting a chant and making the sign of the cross. While the woman next to her in a leopard unitard and high heels held up a sign that said...

Watch out for Isosceles! He no good!

"In all fairness, half of the people down there are *my* family. That's one of the reasons we're on this trip." The man next to the woman shook his head with a chuckle and held out his hand. "Nik Stevens."

Interesting. The name Stevens wasn't Greek, but he'd said his family, so he must be half Greek. Those Greek genes must be strong because he looked like a Greek god.

Mitch shook the man's hand. "Mitch Stone. Nice to meet you."

I smiled on the inside, listening to my own handsome man's deep voice. I was one lucky woman.

"This is my girlfriend, Kalli Ballas." Nik gestured to the woman beside him.

Kalli waved. "I have to say, I'm not a fan of cruises. The thought of being on a boat terrifies me, but the ocean is literally the only way we can spend *any* time alone."

"We know all about that," Mitch said, gesturing to me. "This is my wife, Sunny. I don't have any family around, and Sunny's isn't nearly as big as either of yours, but they are the masters of meddling."

"It's true." I watched the people on the pier become small specks as our cruise ship pulled out to sea. "The only reason they're not here is because they are preoccupied with taking care of our six-month-old son and two-year-old daughter."

"Wow, you have your hands full." Kalli gave one last glance at the disappearing dock before looking back at us. "Anyone up for a drink? I could sure use one."

"You read my mind," I answered.

A funny look swam into her eyes before she smiled a little too wide and led the way.

Shrugging, I followed her over to The Sky Deck, which was a fun looking bar with pop music filtering through the sound system. Our men were already deep in conversation, apparently hitting it off splendidly.

"Ladies and gentleman, welcome." Our bartender set cocktail napkins before us. "Franklin Gibbs at your service, but you can call me Frankie. Everyone else does." He winked. "Anything you want, I can make it. Right, Courtney?"

"You're the man, Frankie." The cocktail waitress sporting jet black hair with green tips, pale purple eyes, and a nose ring let out a little snort and kept walking, but she rolled her eyes at me as she passed by.

I pressed my lips together to stifle a giggle. This cruise was turning out to be entertaining so far.

"What's your pleasure, folks?" The bartender flipped a shaker in the air, catching it expertly.

Frankie was average height with an athletic build, probably in his mid-thirties, sporting short sandy brown hair with longer bangs swept to the side and hazel eyes. I couldn't help but notice his eyelashes were longer than any woman I'd ever seen. He looked like a real charmer, judging by the twinkle in his eyes.

"I'll have a chardonnay." Kalli pulled out a sanitized wipe and ran it over her barstool before she sat.

"A Long Island Iced Tea for me, please." I smiled, sliding the cocktail napkin in front of me.

"Make mine a beer." Mitch tapped the bar.

"Same." Nik shot Frankie a nod.

The men fell into conversation with the bartender, so I grabbed my drink and moved down to sit by Kalli.

"Do you mind?" I asked her first.

"Not at all." She tugged a wipe out of a packet and handed it to me. "I know they're supposed to keep the ship super clean, but all the germs that might be lingering in tiny crevices creep me out."

"Thanks." I took the wipe and ran it over the stool before sitting down. "I have to admit I'm not one who worries too much about those sorts of things." I took a sip of my cocktail and sighed over the tea and spirits combo currently dancing a tango across my tastebuds.

"I wish I could say the same." She shuddered, wiped off the rim of her glass with a napkin three times, and then pulled out a pink collapsible metal straw that looked like a Barbie-sized cane, snapping it into shape. She slipped it inside her wine glass and then took a dainty sip. "I worry way too much about that sort of thing *all* the time."

"That's okay. I'm about as different as they come. A lot of people don't get me, but the ones that matter do." I shrugged. "That's all I care about."

"Same. I'm lucky to have Nik. I didn't want to let him down by saying no to a vacation, but I really don't want to be stuck on a boat in the middle of the ocean."

"Mitch is the same way." I nodded. "It took me forever to convince him we deserved some time alone together. At least we only have one day at sea, and then we will be in Bermuda. I can't wait. The islands look amazing with their pink sand beaches. I find it fascinating that they're all connected by bridges."

"I will be so happy to plant my feet firmly on the ground." Kalli laughed, then looked speculative. "Or submerged volcano, I should say. The coral islands are just a two-hundred-foot layer of thick marine limestone that caps the extinct mountain range, but it's better than floating over a fourteen-thousand-foot drop to the ocean floor."

"Wow, I didn't know that. How cool." I rubbed my hands together. "I have to admit, I love learning about all the legends and myths."

Kalli's smile slipped into a frown. "My family is afraid we will disappear into the Bermuda Triangle, or Isosceles as my Aunt Tasoula calls him." Kalli chuckled while shaking her head. "My family believes in all sorts of legends and myths because of their culture. Even though I'm adopted and was raised in that same culture, I'm firmly grounded in science and facts." She raised her glass in cheers.

I laughed and did the same. "*My* family is the complete opposite." I rolled my eyes. "As a former doctor and a former lawyer, my parents are all about science and facts. My grandmother Gertrude is the only one who believes in the possibility of all sorts of things you can't explain. I take after her."

"I never used to believe in that sort of thing," Kalli ripped her cocktail napkin into tiny pieces as she talked, "but after everything that's happened to me over the past year, I'm starting to." Her purse fell off the back of her chair.

"Here, let me." I bent down and picked it up off the floor.

Suddenly my eyes narrowed into tunnel vision just like they always did when I held a personal item of someone's and had a vision about them. I embodied the woman in the vision and looked out at the world through her eyes. I was standing up in a loft, reaching for a mannequin, when I fell backward over the railing. My arms windmilled when suddenly I hit the floor hard. A sharp pain sliced through my head and my world went black. When I came to, a stunning woman stood over me, patting my cheeks and saying my name.

But her lips weren't moving.

"Sunny, are you okay?" Kalli's voice cut through my thoughts, yanking me back to the present. She helped me up into my chair but didn't let go. Her eyes suddenly widened as her hand gripped my arm.

So, how long have you been able to read minds? I thought.

She gasped and let go of me. Scrubbing her hands with hand sanitizer, she scanned the area around us, looking alarmed. No one was paying any attention. "How did you know?" she whispered.

On a hunch, I reached out and touched her arm again, assuming based on her actions that our contact was how she had heard my thoughts. *Because I'm psychic.* I winked and let a slow smile spread across my face.

This time she didn't pull away as a wide, beaming smile spread across hers.

And just like that, a bond was formed.

~

Kalli

Later that evening, Nik and I headed to dinner to meet Sunny and Mitch. When we'd met them earlier, we'd hit it off so well. Because of that, we'd requested to be seated at the same table for dinner. Luckily, the dining room manager was able to accommodate us. I really liked Sunny and felt better about my quirks after discovering she was psychic. No one knew about my mind-reading ability other than Nik and my best friend, Jaz, back home.

It was nice to be able to share my secret with someone who had a gift of her own.

The main dining room, Maritime Eatery, consisted of a fun island theme with pictures of tropical birds, pink sand beaches, lighthouses, thatch huts, gorgeous flowers, and trees. Jaz insisted on packing for me since I mostly lived in boring—according to Jaz—business suits with my hair pulled back in a chignon. I personally liked the style. It made me feel confident and in control, even though no one would ever guess I designed a lingerie line in the loft of Jaz's clothing boutique.

I tried so hard not to fidget in the seafoam green rayon sundress with matching high heeled slingbacks she'd packed for me. I was thankful it was at least a solid color. I smiled slightly. My best friend knew me well.

Nik squeezed my hand as we headed toward our table. *You look beautiful, Ballas.*

My heart warmed, and my lips tipped up in appreciation as I squeezed his hand back. He loved thinking all sorts of things, knowing I could hear him when we touched, never missing an opportunity to mess with me. But he also *always* made me feel like the most special woman in the world. I felt so lucky to have met him.

My devilish boyfriend had on a pink flamingo silk shirt with linen pants, loafers, and a smug grin. When he was in Detective Stevens mode, he was all business. When he was Nik, he was the nice guy. But tonight, Nikos the Greek was most definitely in attendance and ready to play. I couldn't help but giggle.

Mitch and Sunny arrived at the same time. Mitch was the serious sort, much like me. I could appreciate his pale grey button-down dress shirt, black dress pants, and dress shoes. While Sunny was just like my Nikos: a twinkle in her eye and full of life. She wore a sunflower sundress with a fringed hem and flat leather sandals.

"Good evening, folks. My name is Xavier Walters, and I will be your head waiter. Take a moment to get to know your tablemates, and I'll be around shortly to take your orders. Here is the list of choices for tonight's dinner. If you have any questions, don't hesitate to ask." We all thanked him as he passed out the menus with a big smile, revealing perfectly straight white teeth beneath full lips. He looked at us with kind brown eyes behind small glasses, then tipped his gleaming bald head slightly before walking away.

"What a lovely man." Sunny's smile was as bright as the flower petals on her dress. "Isn't this room fabulous?"

"It looks like paradise." I scanned the menu, sitting in the seat next to her, then looked around and listened to the sounds of clanking silverware and laughter. The smells wafting through the room were heaven-sent.

"It's okay," said a distinguished looking man at our table with an empty seat beside him. He was probably in his fifties, with salt and pepper hair slicked back. He swirled the ice in his rocks glass before taking a noisy gulp. "I've seen better."

"Interesting. And you are...?" said a much older, equally distinguished looking man who sat across from him. His steel grey hair was parted on the side and precisely trimmed, and he sported a matching raised eyebrow.

"Baron Von Wielig." The younger man held out his hand.

The older man shook his hand firmly as they gave

each other the once over. "Milton Dubois, and this is my wife, Mavis."

"It's a pleasure to meet you." The petite woman bowed her head slightly, her snow-white, chicly cut and styled hair revealing huge diamond earrings that peeked out from beneath and reflected the light like a kaleidoscope.

"The pleasure's all mine." Baron's gaze traveled over to our side of the table, lingering on Sunny and then me. "What lovely creatures do we have here?"

I felt my ears heat and saw Sunny's face grow pink as her gaze met mine. I cleared my throat and finally responded. "Kalli Ballas."

"And I'm, um...um..." Sunny frowned and then laughed. "Sunny Meadows. Don't know where my head is at."

Mitch grunted. "Sunny Stone you mean."

"Oh, right." She laughed again, slapping her forehead. "Pregnancy brain. My mind still isn't right since having my second baby six months ago."

"Six months ago?" Baron's voice purred. "Well, you look fantastic."

"Yes, my *wife* sure does," Mitch ground out.

"And you are?" Baron's lips twitched.

A muscle in Mitch's jaw bulged. "Detective Stone."

"You can call him Mitch." Sunny gave him a stern look. "No work on this trip, remember?"

"You're a detective?" Nik's black eyebrows shot up. "Isn't that something? I'm a detective as well." He glanced at Baron. "Detective Stevens."

"*Nik* won't be working on this trip either," I said firmly and gave Sunny a conspiratorial nod.

"Unfortunately, I'm always working." Baron shrugged. "I don't mind. I don't have a family, and I love my work. It serves me well." He shifted in an obviously calculated way so that his suit coat sleeve raised up, revealing a very expensive looking watch, or *time piece* as they say.

"Hmmm, *we're* from a long line of Dubois. Old money, you know. Been around for centuries." Milton raised his chin a notch. "What is it you do?"

"I'm a self-made businessman." Baron sat up straighter. "I deal in art. In fact, a private collection of one of my clients will be on display during this cruise with an auction on our last day at sea. You won't want to miss that."

"Don't you worry." Milton's eyes reduced to slits. "I don't miss much. Do I, dear?" His shrewd gaze slid to his wife.

"No, my Milton certainly does not." She looked at Sunny and me. "Enough talk about all our men. I want to know what these lovely ladies do. I chair several organizations in our social circle, as well as run many charities. How do you both spend your days?"

I swallowed hard and stared at Sunny, my mouth going dry.

She beamed proudly, not seeming affected in the least. "I read people's fortunes." She leaned forward and said with a devilish grin. "I'm psychic."

"Oh, my word." Mavis clapped her hands. "How exciting. Will you read my fortune this week?"

"Well, I did promise my husband that I wouldn't work either," she eyed Mitch who arched a brow at her, waiting for something, "but I might be able to squeeze in a little reading when he's in the ship's cigar lounge or golfing on the island." She peeked back at him, biting her bottom lip.

And there it was. Cigars and golf upped the ante. The corners of Mitch's mouth tipped up ever so slightly as he lifted his hands in a helpless gesture but then winked at her.

"It's a date." Sunny handed her phone to Mavis. "If you would add your number to my contacts, we'll set something up."

"I'm old school, honey. I can barely use my own phone." Mavis handed the phone back to Sunny and wrote her number on a napkin, then slid it across the table. "That's how we did it in the old days, and then waited with bated breath for our beau to call. It didn't take my Milton more than an hour." She winked.

Sunny laughed. "No worries. I've got you covered."

"Great, now that that's settled," Mavis looked at me, "what is it that you do, my dear?"

"I design clothing," I said carefully.

"Oh, how wonderful." Mavis beamed. "I would love to see your collection."

"Sexy lingerie," Nik added with a gleam in his eyes. "She just finished her spring line of Kalli Originals. Maybe she can squeeze in something special for you this week, too." He winked at me as well, but his eyes were full of mischief.

I stepped on his foot beneath our table, and he let out a little yelp. "Please don't feel obligated to buy—"

"I adore lingerie." Mavis blew her husband a kiss. "Even at our age, one must always work at keeping their marriage alive. Isn't that right, darling?"

"A happy wife is a happy life. And it's never work with you, lovie." Milton kissed his wife's hand, and she blushed.

"Well, all right, then." I took out my phone. "I guess you'd better give me your number as well. Looks like my guy will be indulging in cigars and golf as well."

Nik grinned wide at Mitch.

I shook my head, trying not to laugh. Sunny handed me the napkin and I entered Mavis's number into my phone just as Brie and Haden Gray, the cruise photographers, stopped by our table.

The cruise guide said they were around to take photos whenever anyone got on or off the ship. At excursions. After dinner. Candid shots. Formal night. They pretty much were around to capture every moment.

"Anyone up for some dinner shots with your new friends?" Brie asked. She was tall and fit with jet black hair pulled back in a high ponytail and sparkling emerald green eyes full of enthusiasm.

"Sure," Sunny said. "I love pictures."

"Great. If you four could lean in." Haden pointed to Mitch, Sunny, Nik, and me.

We did as he requested.

"Say scallywag." Brie smiled, showing all her teeth.

We couldn't help but smile back and comply with her wishes.

Haden raised his camera then snapped a shot. He was equally tall and fit with dark blond hair pulled back in a manbun, a tightly cropped beard, and thoughtful deep blue eyes.

"Okay, now. How about the rest of you?" Brie turned to Baron, Milton, and Mavis.

Baron's phone went off obnoxiously loud.

Milton's face transformed into a disapproving sour pucker.

Mavis yelled, "Scallywag."

Brie shrugged.

Haden snapped off a shot.

Baron's phone kept ringing. Several heads in the dining room turned, but Baron ignored them. He looked at the caller ID and frowned. "Excuse me, folks. I have to take this." He answered the phone, and his frown deepened. He looked around as if searching for someone or something.

I glanced in that direction but had no clue what he'd been looking for.

He stood abruptly and walked out of the dining room without another word.

What a strange first day. I suddenly wondered how far *Isosceles'* reach might be, and what other mysteries were in store for us.

2

___

SUNNY

"That felt amazing," I said to Kalli as we sipped rum punch from our lounge chairs beneath our umbrella by the pool, with her handy dandy pink collapsible metal straws clinking against our glasses.

Turns out she had two.

It amazed me that New York City was still chilly this time of year, yet the closer we got to Bermuda, the warmer the temperature became. Today was a sunny day, so the temperature was perfect. I'd had a full-body, deep-tissue massage, and my post-pregnancy body was humming its appreciation.

"My guy, Ivan, is a magician, I swear." I stretched like my mischievous cat, Morty, and fairly certain I even purred a little.

My mind immediately went to my family, and I sighed, the yummy cocktail turning sour in my stomach. I could only imagine what sort of drama was unfolding back home. Morty, short for immortal, was staying with Great Grandma Tootsie because it was clear from the moment they'd met, they had a special bond. She was the one-hundred-year-old cook at Divine Inspiration, my parents' inn on the outskirts of

Divinity, along with her sous chefs, Granny Gert and her best friend Fiona.

The Tasty Trio caused as much mischief as Morty on a daily basis, but they all promised to be on their best behavior while my parents watched our children. I certainly hoped they were because this vacation was long overdue, and I didn't want anything to ruin it. I chewed my bottom lip, thinking my family wasn't the problem this time. I couldn't shake the nagging feeling of doom that had settled in my gut from the moment I'd stepped foot on this ship.

I had learned the hard way to always trust my gut.

"A facial was about all I could handle," Kalli's voice broke through my gloomy thoughts. "Even then, I couldn't relax." She tipped her sunhat further back to see me. "My girl, Natalia, kept thinking in great detail about the fight she'd had with her boyfriend the night before. Speaking of magicians, Lance is a *real* one who performs on board. Apparently, he cheated on her with his assistant, Chee Chee."

I adjusted my sunglasses and gaped at Kalli. "Well, that definitely could not have been relaxing. What did you do?"

"Slipped up and told Natalia to move on before Lance could play any more tricks on her." Kalli slathered her pale skin with more sunscreen.

I laughed. "Oh, my. What on earth did *she* do?"

"Asked me how I could possibly know that and accused me of being friends with his floozy assistant in trying to break them up." Kalli shook her head. "I was only trying to help, but I think I made things worse. Poor girl. I don't think this is the last we'll see of him cheating on her. He'll just find someone new on board."

"I hear you on being distracted. It's hard with our

gifts. I not only can predict the future, but I can also see the past, especially when touching the person or holding one of their items close." I looked around to make sure no one could hear us. "I saw Ivan and Natalia talking together before they took us to separate rooms. During my massage, I had a vision of his past. He has been pining away for that girl for years, and she has no idea. They both have such beautiful features, they would make a stunning couple."

"Aww, that's sweet." Kalli looked at me with hope in her eyes. She was such a genuine, nice person, I really liked her. "Maybe they'll eventually find each other," she added dreamily. "I just love a happy ending."

"I'm not sure if a happy ending is in the cards for them because I didn't see the future. Maybe I could..." I shook my head hard to rid my mind of the crazy impulses to help that kept flooding my brain. "We're *not* here to play matchmaker or fix people's problems." I nodded firmly, more as a reminder to myself not to get caught up in drama. "We're here to relax, no matter how hard that might be. We've earned this."

Kali was already nodding. "Yes, we have. I'm beginning to think we're both way too nice." Kalli stared off in the distance and squinted as if to see better. "Oh, boy. Speaking of problems."

I followed her gaze and saw Baron in a heated conversation with a young woman. She wore a large sunhat and glasses, but there was no mistaking the long curly dark brown hair that fell to her waist.

"Who is that?" Kalli pointed. "I haven't seen her before, but she doesn't seem too happy to be talking to him."

"I don't know." I shrugged, fighting the urge to go see if she was okay. There was something about the man that I didn't trust. "But earlier, on my way to the spa, I saw them come out of Baron's room together and then head in separate directions."

"Interesting. Lover's tiff? He's a lot older than her." Kalli placed her straw between her lips and sipped her rum punch speculatively.

"That doesn't matter to some people, and there is the fact that he's rich." I sipped my own drink, studying the couple.

"Rich and full of himself." Kalli's nose wrinkled and her lips pursed. "I have to say I'm not a fan of his."

Mystery Girl stomped her foot, her hands flying a mile a minute as she talked, then she stormed out of the pool area causing quite the scene. Baron looked flustered, pausing when he saw us watching him, then he purposely stood up straighter. He adjusted the towel around his neck, shot us a wave with a beaming smile, and then headed off in the opposite direction as if nothing had happened.

"Here we go again, getting ourselves involved in drama." Kalli raised her hands, palms up. "I can't seem to help myself."

"Same." I laughed. "Even after I promised Mitch I wouldn't."

The cruise director, Diana North, had dark luscious hair and a body most women would kill for. She reminded me of my best friend Jo, who looked like an Amazon goddess, which made me miss home. Diana's sultry voice that could talk pretty much anyone into doing anything came over the loudspeaker, stating that fitness director, Dallas Skinner, was about to start water calisthenics and was looking for some new volunteers.

Dallas, with his wild blond curly hair, tight speedo, and massive smile that revealed blazing white teeth, started scanning the deck. His gaze stopped on us, and his eyes widened with brimming excitement that said…

Fresh meat.

He started dancing his way over to us while singing through his headset for all to hear, "Slide to the left." *Clap, clap, clap.* "Slide to the right." *Clap, clap, clap.* "Come on, ladies." *Clap, clap, clap.* "Don't be uptight."

I giggled and started clapping and singing along, my mood brightening instantly.

Kalli's face paled even more as she looked at me, horrified.

Brie and Haden captured every moment on camera, of course.

Dallas cast an imaginary fishing pole at me, yanked the pole back, and pretended to reel me in. I couldn't help playing along. I jerked forward as if he'd hooked me and pretended to put up a struggle by stepping forward then stumbling back a few times.

Kalli stood, held up her fingers as if they were scissors, then shook her head no at Dallas as she clipped the imaginary fishing line and pulled me back to our chairs. I shrugged helplessly at Dallas and mouthed, *Next time.*

"We should go." Kalli looked at me, her pale face registering her discomfort. "Ready to find the guys?"

"Sure thing," I said gently, giving her an encouraging smile and vowing to get her to loosen up by the end of the cruise. I looked at the clock on the wall. "They should be done with the cigar lounge and casino by now."

"Sounds like a plan to me." She gathered her things. "I'm *betting* they are staying out of trouble much better than we are."

Kalli

"Weren't they spectacular?" I asked as we left the theater later that evening and headed to our favorite lounge, The Wheelhouse.

A band played in the corner and the interior had a rustic ambiance, with wooden ship wheels mounted throughout. The Sky Deck bar would be too chilly now that the sun had set, and frankly, staring out at the vast ocean with no land in sight freaked me out.

I never should have watched *Titanic* before setting sail.

"Angela Rose and Elton Marshall have amazing voices, and their acting isn't bad, either," Sunny agreed.

"I personally think Elton steals the show," Mavis said from behind us as she walked beside her husband. "He looks like a young Sean Connery. Milton, here, has a thing for Angela, though." Mavis winked. "He always has been a sucker for a theater gal, especially one who looks like Meryl Streep in her prime."

"No one holds a candle to you, darling." Milton bowed his head and kissed the back of her hand in a gallant fashion.

"Such a charming man I married." She beamed, but then her smile slipped as we entered the lounge.

Baron's voice carried across the room as he boomed, "This round is on me."

"People with *real* money don't boast about it." Milton looked down his nose at the self-made businessman.

Baron handed a drink to a woman I recognized from my shopping adventure before dinner. Cara

Carmichael. She was short and curvy with deep dimples and wavy shoulder length auburn hair. I'd met her in Cruise Wave Couture, the clothing boutique on board. I was checking out the product line to gather ideas for Jaz's clothing line as well as gain inspiration for my next lingerie collection. I'd made the mistake of thinking Cara worked there.

When I asked her a question, she informed me she was the art auctioneer for the upcoming show on board. She was only in the store to shop as well for a few items she hadn't anticipated needing. In the end, I helped her choose the correct size lingerie. It amazed me how so many women didn't realize their true size in undergarments.

I glanced over at Baron. He and Cara looked pretty chummy, and it made me wonder if Mystery Girl was out of the picture now. It wouldn't surprise me after their heated argument at the pool earlier. Cara was still younger than Baron, but much closer to his age than the younger woman had been. Although, if she was the auctioneer for his client's private art collection, I would think them getting involved would be a conflict of interest.

"Aren't the drinks free anyway?" Sunny brought my attention back to our group and the free round Baron had bought.

"Only if you purchase the unlimited drink package," Mitch clarified, holding up his beer. "Which we did." He winked.

"Same." Nik clinked his highball glass to Mitch's longneck bottle.

They both let out a hearty laugh.

Spotting someone across the room, Nik waved an older woman over. She reminded me of his ma who had raised him on her own after his parents divorced and his Scandinavian pop had moved back to England. His ma, Chloe, had never remarried, but now that Nik was a grown man, she was dating his captain.

I may be adopted and Nik only half-Greek, but our mamas were Greek enough for the both of us and wanted a big wedding and a chariot full of grandbabies.

The older woman joined our circle. "Well, hello again, you two." She smiled and looked at Mitch and Nik with kind brown eyes, patting her dark brown curled and set head of hair.

"This is Maria Giovanni. Mitch and I had the pleasure of meeting her at the cigar bar and the casino earlier." Nik slipped his arm around her petite shoulders and introduced her to the group.

Everyone welcomed her warmly.

"My late husband, Dante, loved his cigars and gambling. We had already booked this cruise for our anniversary when he got sick and passed away a year ago. I made him a promise on his deathbed that I would still go and do all the things we had planned. So, I had a cigar and I gambled in his honor." She raised her hands. "I don't see what the fuss is all about, but it did make me think of him and bring a smile to my lips." She made the sign of the cross and kissed her fingers.

I liked her already.

I could see my own ma doing exactly that if anything ever happened to my pop. Although, Aunt Tasoula would insist on coming along, and then all sorts of chaos would ensue. Talk about getting into trouble.

The Dynamic Duo were the queens of disaster.

"I think it's wonderful that you came on this vacation still." Sunny smiled with kindness and warmth emanating from her. Just one more reason why I liked her so much. "Just know you're not alone," she added. "You have us." She swept her hand at the group. "We're all here for you, and we'll help you get through the trip making wonderful new memories. Isn't that right, Mitch?"

"Of course." He nodded once, slipping his arm around his wife, then his gaze swept the room the same that Nik's had.

Always on alert.

I took a sip of my chardonnay, through my personal straw of course, as everyone fell into conversation, listening to the classic soft rock music being sung by the band in the corner. Suddenly, Sunny tapped my arm. I looked at her and she pointed to the doorway exiting the lounge.

My gaze followed suit.

Mystery Girl had her head bent close to Lance the magician, and the next thing I knew, they disappeared...

Together.

My jaw fell open, and I tipped my head toward Sunny. "What do you think it means?"

"Nothing good." She looked over to Baron, who was still listening to Cara, but his narrowed eyes were fixed on the empty doorway.

"That's what I was afraid of." I hadn't had a good feeling since my family had invaded the dock back in New York City.

Something told me *Isosceles* was the least of our worries.

3

—————

SUNNY

The next morning, we arrived in Bermuda at the Royal Naval Dockyard. Mitch and I stood on the upper deck, watching the ship dock. It was early morning and the sun had just come up. The day looked like it was going to be a beautiful one.

"Wow, Bermuda is stunning." I looked around in wonder. "I feel like we're visiting a small slice of paradise with its turquoise waters and tangerine sunsets."

"It sure is." Mitch rubbed my back. "I have to admit, you made a good choice in picking these islands for our vacation."

According to the brochure I read, there were seven main islands clustered together in the shape of a fishhook and connected by bridges. The largest island was only fourteen miles long and one mile wide, with its highest peak only around two-hundred-fifty feet. The islands didn't have any rivers or lakes, but they were surrounded by the ocean and fringed with gorgeous coral reefs. The soil was shallow but that didn't stop flowering shrubs like bougainvillea, Easter lilies, oleander, hibiscus, and poinsettia from growing.

"Are you sure you don't mind Nik and me playing the Port Royal Golf Course?" Mitch peeked down at me with those grey eyes of his, stormy and full of concern.

"I promise you that I don't mind. Kalli and I want to walk through the pink sand at Horseshoe Bay Beach, and then we'll shop at the Bermuda Café Market, followed by a traditional afternoon tea with sandwiches and scones. You know you guys wouldn't be into any of that. Besides, our activities will only take up half the day. Then the four of us can visit Gibb's Hill Lighthouse together. Did you know that it's one of the world's oldest cast iron lighthouses and it's supposed to have incredible views?"

"I did not." His lips tipped up slightly at the corners. "Did *you* know you can sip Rum Swizzle at an English pub here? As a self-governing British overseas territory, I heard that Bermuda has some of the best English Pubs."

I laughed. "Okay, okay. You guys go to the lighthouse with us, and we'll go to the pub with you two. Deal?"

"Deal." He leaned down and kissed me softly on the lips, and the butterflies danced in my stomach even after all these years.

Nik and Kalli joined us on the deck.

"You ready to hit the links, buddy?" Nik swung an imaginary golf club.

"You don't have to ask me twice, partner." Mitch rubbed his hands together.

It was clear the men had formed a bond as quickly as Kalli and I had. They had the whole detective thing in common, while we had our *gifts*. And we all had crazy families we had to deal with. It was nice having people we enjoyed sharing in this experience with us.

Nik winked at Kalli then raised his hands in question.

She laughed and just shook her head. "Boys will be boys, I guess. Go on with you, then. Sunny and I have plenty of things to keep us busy."

"Like touring the dramatic Crystal Caves followed by an evening sail into the Bermuda Triangle on a glass-bottom boat? We could skip everything and do that instead. Who's game?" I grinned wide with raised eyebrows in question.

Everyone else frowned.

"I take that as a hard no." I shrugged. No one wanted anything to do with exploring the mystery of the infamous Devil's triangle. "In that case, you boys better get going." I shooed Mitch off. "We have a full day of other fun activities lined up."

"We'll meet you after our afternoon tea," Kalli said and gave Nik a kiss goodbye.

The men left to catch their ride, and we headed off the ship for a day of fun in the sun, with a quick stop for photos from Brie and Haden, or course. The sky was clear, not a cloud in sight. There wasn't even a sea breeze. It was kind of eerie how still everything was.

Like the calm before a storm.

I shook off the annoying sense of doom that still wouldn't go away, refusing to let it ruin my vacation as I enjoyed my surroundings. Palm, pine, casuarina, and mangrove trees were found on most of the islands, as well as a number of migratory birds, lizards, and frogs.

That was the extent of the wildlife, thank goodness.

We walked along the shore, and I carried my sandals, letting my bare feet shuffle through the pink sand crystals. "I feel like we're in a world of pink glitter."

"It is rather pretty, isn't it? Like some of the material I use in my designs. It gets its color from pulverized coral and shells." Kalli smiled wistfully, then her smile slipped as she inspected the sand closer. "Though I wouldn't take my shoes off if you paid me. Ocean water is dirty enough, but sand is much worse. At least water born bacteria dies off and disappears rather quickly, but microbes tend to get trapped in the sand and take much longer to decay." She shuddered, stepping carefully on top of the sand with her sneaker encased feet.

"Ew, I never thought of it that way." I dropped my sandals on the beach and slid my feet into them.

She blinked. "Oh, I'm so sorry. Just ignore me. I tend to get caught up in my head about stuff like that. I really need to stay off the Internet."

"It's okay." I laughed. "The sand was getting hot anyway." I shielded my eyes and looked off toward the row of shops, then glanced at Kalli whose eyes lit up. "You thinking what I'm thinking?"

"Oh, yeah. Forget hitting the links. I'm ready to hit the racks." She forged ahead, picking up the pace, and led the way straight to a row of adorable boutiques.

I hurried to catch up.

The buildings all had pastel-colored exteriors with white limestone roofs that had stepped edges and charming, picturesque designs. Tall, narrow windows caught the island breezes and managed the heat, and there were lush gardens with well-maintained lawns everywhere. I could appreciate the islands' history and cultural influences.

"Did you know Bermuda primarily relies on rainwater harvesting to obtain its drinking water?" Kalli's face came alive with excitement whenever she opened a filing cabinet in that smart brain of hers and spit out random facts. She pointed up. "That's why the roof of this building is designed this way, so it can collect rainwater, which is then stored in tanks for consumption. Some water is also sourced from underground lenses and desalination plants, which convert seawater into freshwater since they don't have any natural freshwater sources on the islands."

"Fascinating." I rubbed my hands together, getting excited to see the treasures inside.

Walking through the front door, we ran into Mavis and Milton Dubois.

"What do you think, ladies?" Mavis held up a dress.

"It's lovely, Mavis. As playful and colorful as the island itself." Kalli touched the silky fabric.

"You should get one for yourself, my dear."

"Oh, well, I'm more of a solid material kind of girl."

"All the more reason to step out of your comfort zone and get one." I shot Mavis a conspiratorial wink.

Kalli nodded once. "You know what? You're right." She started browsing the racks.

"Well, I, for one, am going with traditional Bermuda shorts, paired with a jacket and tie, of course." Milton admired his jacket in a mirror.

"Of course, darling. I would expect nothing less from you." Mavis beamed at her husband.

"Mitch would be all about the jacket and tie, but I'm not so sure I could get him into a pair of those shorts." I giggled.

"Nik would gladly wear the shorts, but he would ditch the jacket and tie, pairing them with some outlandish, colorful shirt, no doubt."

"Let's buy them a pair anyway." I loved shopping for other people.

I stepped up to the counter behind a man with gold and white hair. He was buying a pair of water shoes, telling the clerk it was his first cruise. He wanted to try some new adventures, but he wasn't so sure he had the confidence. Art galleries were more his speed.

Speaking of art, my eyes were drawn to the wall behind the clerk while I waited my turn. "Oooh, for myself I want to buy some prints." I pointed at the wall to Kalli. "Just look at that artwork. The details are extraordinary."

"I agree," the guy ahead of me said and added a print to his purchases as well.

"That's a fine choice, Mr. Overton." The cashier handed him a receipt.

"If cheap, amateur work is your thing," Baron Von Wielig boomed as he entered the store with what had to be the magician's assistant, Chee Chee, on his arm. There was no mistaking her huge head of teased bottle-blond hair and Dolly Parton measurements I'd seen on posters in the theater.

My eyes sprang wide then shot to Kalli's. I casually touched her arm. *First, he's with Mystery Woman. Then, he's with Cara Carmichael, the art auctioneer. Now, he shows up with Chee Chee, the magician's assistant? This guy sure makes the rounds and doesn't seem to have a type. They're all so different.*

Milton rolled his eyes. "I thought you were going on an excursion today?"

"Bah, the guide is some environmental nut. He got all bent out of shape over a little piece of trash I dropped on the ground. I was going to pick it up, but he beat me to it. So, we decided to shop instead." Baron looked around with an unimpressed expression on his face.

Milton's mouth puckered. "Come along, Mavis. It's time we take our leave. I suddenly have a sour stomach." He left their items behind without purchasing them and walked toward the door with a confused-looking Mavis.

"Don't forget to stop by my client's art auction tomorrow," Baron hollered after him. "Then you'll see what *real* talent is all about."

"I'll have to check my schedule. You know how it is." Milton thrust his nose in the air. "Come along, lovie. We have places to be." Mavis shrugged then took his arm, waved to us, and they waltzed their way out the door.

Mystery Girl walked into the shop with Lance the magician. I recognized his blond-haired, green-eyed Hollywood looks from his poster hanging outside the theater as well. Lance's eyes widened at Chee Chee, and Mystery Girl's eyes narrowed at Baron. Chee Chee scowled, Baron set his jaw, and all four left the building.

"What just happened?" I asked.

"Apparently, more than just trouble in paradise." Kalli watched them argue as they marched down the street until they branched off in opposite directions.

"That's what I'm afraid of." The sense of doom in my stomach built to hurricane level, ready to be unleashed.

Something told me none of us would remain unscathed by the storm that was brewing.

~

Kalli

In the middle of the night, I woke up after rolling off the bed and hitting my head. I sat up and rubbed my scalp. Nik reached out and helped me up, looking at me in confusion. *What is happening?*

His thoughts mirrored my own. "Well, at least I have one question answered. I can still read minds." I grabbed onto a shelf that was bolted to the wall just as the speaker came on in our room.

"This is Captain Heather Hughes speaking. We're experiencing a bit of rough seas. Stay in your cabins. No need to panic, folks. This ship is built for storms like these, but we're not taking a chance with anyone's safety."

"You don't have to tell me twice." Nik stumbled across the room and wrapped his arms around me to grip the shelf and keep me safe.

"I don't like this one bit," I said. "I'm afraid of the triangle but not for the superstitious reason's my family is."

"It *is* kind of freaky that so many ships and aircraft have gone missing as early as 1609," he pointed out. "Like more than fifty ships and twenty airplanes to put things in perspective. That's a lot. Even Shakespear wrote The Tempest after being inspired by The Devil's Triangle." His brilliant blue eyes stared at me with genuine concern. "What if there is something to the myths?"

I held on tight to the shelf as another wave rocked the boat hard. "You sound like my family. They really think The Bermuda triangle is like the lost continent of Atlantis. They think paranormal activity is the cause. Or time travel portals that suck objects into other dimensions. Some of them even believe extraterrestrials abducted whole ships, planes, and people who vanished without a trace." I shook my head and looked up at him. "I think they're all nuts."

"I'm not so sure." Nik chewed the inside of his cheek, looking thoughtful. "How do you explain the strange happenings in the triangle of ocean between

Bermuda, Puerto Rico, and Florida. Remember Maria the widow and Elton the entertainer?"

I nodded.

"Well, they played golf with Mitch and me today. Our excursion guide, Simon, was telling us about the mystery around the triangle. The USS Cyclops was a navy cargo ship with more than three hundred people on board, never to be seen again. Then there was Flight 19, the leader of five navy bombers on a practice run. They ended up in the triangle after their compass malfunctioned and ran out of gas because they couldn't find their way out." His eyes locked on mine.

I waited patiently for him to continue. He loved a good dramatic story and trying to prove he was right.

"After that, the rescue team who went in search of them on the same day they disappeared never came back. Even Columbus recorded weird lights, malfunctioning compasses, and a burst of flame." He raised his hands in the air. "How do you explain no one sending out a signal for help, either?"

"Well, most of these occurrences happened a long time ago before faster warning times when storms roll in." I shrugged.

"That's true." He nodded; his detective side peaked with my newfound knowledge thanks to Sunny.

"You know," I continued, excited to share. "Tropical cyclones can occur rapidly, causing downdrafts of cold air which can hit the water surface like a bomb."

"I've heard of that." He scrubbed a hand over his heavily whiskered jaw. "Those old ships would sink instantaneously from the outward explosion."

"Not to mention," I said a little louder so as not to be outdone, "large fields of methane gases can bubble and sink a ship by decreasing the density of water to the point where it can't support a ship. They're called mud volcanoes."

He wrinkled his forehead. "Oh, I didn't know that." Nik paused and studied me. "How on earth do you know all of that?"

"What can I say? I like to read." I couldn't keep the grin off my face. I loved this man with all my heart. "And, well, Sunny told me some of those things while we were walking the beach today. Don't worry I kept my shoes on."

"I never doubted that." He winked and his crooked, sexy grin made my insides tingle. "Did she tell you the Gulf Stream is a major current, acting like a river within an ocean? So, if something sinks, it would quickly be dispersed and never found by rescue teams."

"She did. And I also read that The Bermuda Triangle is one of only two places where a compass points to true north instead of magnetic north. So, you see? Mystery solved."

A surge of water hit the boat and we lost our grip, flying across the room and landing on the bed.

Nik looked at me with concern. "I hope for our sake you're right." He grabbed my hand and pulled me into the bathroom where we both got in the shower, fully clothed, to ride out the storm. He held me in his arms. *This is not how I envisioned our vacation.*

"Me, neither. When we get out of here—because I refuse to die and spend my afterlife in Davy Jones's locker—we are going to finish the construction of knocking down the wall between our apartments." I hugged Nik tighter. "No more putting off moving in together. Our current situation is proof that procrastination is never a good thing. Besides, the partially demolished wall between our apartments is driving me crazy."

"Agreed." He hugged me back and didn't let go. *I love you, Ballas.*

"Ditto." I rested my cheek against his chest and settled in.

What felt like hours later, the boat finally calmed down. My stomach was in my throat. I felt so seasick, but I was grateful to get out of the shower. The loudspeaker came on once more, and the captain came over the radio again.

"Good morning, folks. A tropical cyclone swept through the area and pulled us off track, but we made it through the storm and are now back on course. You can all say you've experienced The Bermuda Triangle and lived to tell about it." She laughed as if trying to make light of the situation, but I could hear the relief in her voice. "Today is your final day at sea before we reach port in New York City tomorrow morning. Feel free to leave your cabins and enjoy the rest of the cruise."

"Ma is going to freak out," Nik said.

"Ditto, and Aunt Tasoula will never let me hear the end of Isosceles being no good." I blew out a long, slow breath and stretched my aching muscles. "Are you tired? We've pretty much been up most of the night."

"No, I'm somehow energized." He looked at me and the twinkle was back in his gorgeous blue eyes. "What if we didn't make it out, and this is an alternate universe we're living in."

"Don't even get me started, Detective." I poked him in the chest.

"Hey, it could happen, Ballas." He winked. "As long

as I'm by your side, I don't care what universe I'm living in."

"Nice save." I smiled. "I would kill for a cup of tea."

"Coffee sounds great to me."

We got dressed and headed up to the top deck to watch the sun fully rise. Sunny and Mitch were already up there.

"You couldn't sleep, either?" I asked.

"Hazards of parenthood. Sleepless nights and early mornings." Sunny beamed. "But I love it."

"What a crazy night," Mitch said. "The triangle is on the other side of Bermuda than our ship was docked on. It's crazy how the current pulled us this far off course."

"I know, right?" Nik rubbed his shoulder. "We took some bumps for sure. Ended up in the shower just to keep from being thrown about the room."

"Same here." Mitch grinned. "Logical minds think alike."

They fist-bumped.

Sunny and I rolled our eyes.

"I'm going to get some tea. Want to join me?" I asked her.

"You read my mind." Her eyes twinkled.

This time it didn't freak me out.

We headed to Java Junction, placed our orders, and had just found a table when suddenly an alarm went off. A page went out over the loudspeaker for Mr. Mob, but I knew from my extensive research on cruise ships, that meant man overboard. The boat started to slow immediately and would take six minutes to come to a complete stop, which would be one mile away from the man overboard spot.

The chances of survival were not good when that happened.

"What on earth is happening now?" Sunny asked, looking around.

There was nothing but blue ocean in every direction. The sun was up and there was no land in sight. We looked over the rail on the side of the boat and saw the rescue rafts pull away.

"Someone fell overboard by the sound of it," Nik said, echoing my thoughts.

"Or jumped," Mitch added.

"Or was pushed." Sunny lifted her hands when all our eyes settled on her.

Everyone waited and watched for what felt like forever until finally the rescue boat returned. We were told the person was brought straight to the medical center. Speculation ran rampant about who it was and the state of the person's condition.

No one seemed to want to leave until we found out what exactly had happened.

After some time had passed with passengers waiting anxiously, Captain Heather Hughes, First Officer Tyrone Johnson, and Security Officer Justin Cho appeared on deck. The captain took the microphone from Diana North, the Cruise Director, and looked out over the packed deck with a serious expression before finally raising the microphone.

"Attention everyone. Captain Hughes here again. Unfortunately, I have some grave news. Baron Von Wielig is dead. The incident does not look to be an accident or a suicide." She paused a beat. "There is evidence that he was murdered."

Murmurs of alarm rang out among the crowd.

"I know the news is unsettling, but rest assured, there will be law and order on my ship. Settle in and take advantage of our facilities because you may be here a while. The ship is on lockdown, and no one is allowed to leave. FBI Agent Amy Randolph has been called in to help my team in the investigation, and everyone will be questioned. Your cooperation and patience in this matter is greatly appreciated. Thank you." She handed the microphone to her first mate to answer any questions while she and her security officer left the deck.

I groaned. "I am never taking a cruise again."

"How long do you think we'll be out here?" Mitch asked, looking concerned. "I don't like the idea of being away from the kids for long."

"Me either," Sunny said, "but what can we do?"

Nik looked at Mitch. "I say we do our own investigating. I don't like the idea that a killer is still on board this ship."

A killer was something I could believe in, and suddenly that thought was more terrifying than Isosceles could ever be.

4

SUNNY

"**W**ell, fiddle dee dee. Your story is all over the news. First, the Devil's triangle tried to sink your ship, and now there's been a murder? Why, your poor mother nearly fainted after a fit of the vapors when she heard the news. Good thing your father's a doctor." A pause filled the line briefly. "Are you sure you're okay, honey?" Granny Gert asked through the earpiece of my cell phone.

It was so good to hear a voice from home. "Yes, Granny. Mitch and I are fine. Just a few bumps and bruises from being tossed about in the shower."

"Oh, my stars. Well, that doesn't sound like fun."

I held the phone to my ear as I stood on the top deck, moving around to try for a better signal. You'd never know we just went through a storm. The sun was shining bright in a clear, blue sky with calms seas and no breeze whatsoever. There wasn't any land in sight, but we weren't so far out that cell service was impossible. "I can't talk long. The roaming charges are going to break my bank."

Granny tsked. "You should have gotten the travel pass through your phone carrier. That's what Captain Walker and I did on our last cruise." Granny was a good ten years older than Grady, but he adored her. Ever since he'd retired from the police force, they'd been going on one vacation after another.

"I didn't plan on calling anyone, but I knew the story would break and you all would be worried. I tried Mother, but she didn't pick up. Tell everyone we're fine. We'll just be delayed a little longer. I hope that's okay." The ship had an app where you could text and call other passengers on board, but making calls to the US required being in reach of a cell tower and the connection was spotty at best.

"Don't you worry about that. Your parents are in heaven spoiling their grandchildren. Little Martina is only two and already taking charge of baby River. Such a serious little girl. Vivian is teaching her things well advanced for her age, and she's soaking it up like a sponge. And River, oh my word, that boy doesn't have a care in the world, just like his mama. Donald is happy as a clam being a grandfather, singing and dancing around like a fool—your mother's words, not mine—giving her more gray hairs by the minute. They've never been happier, my dear."

"What about the inn?"

"Great Grandma Tootsie and Morty, Fiona and Harry, and the captain and I are holding down the fort while you and Mitch are gone. I'll have some comfort cookies waiting for you in my favorite pumpkin cookie jar when you get back." Granny Gert had a cookie for everything. "Now stop worrying," her voice lowered a smidgeon as she added, "and try to stay out of trouble, dear."

My grandmother knew me well.

"I don't look for trouble, Gran, honestly. But I swear I'm a magnet for murder. I can't even take a vacation without someone dying. This time I'm not the one doing the snooping." Not yet anyway. "Mitch and Nik can't turn their detective hats off apparently."

"Who's Nik?"

"Detective Nik Stevens and his lovely girlfriend, Kalli Ballas. I'm so excited to have made new friends on this trip, Gran. And guess what?"

"What, dear? Don't keep me in suspense. My psychic abilities aren't as developed as yours. I have to say, I do see signs of psychic ability in little River already. Tina, I'm afraid, is a clone of her daddy with no gift other than her precious self."

"Well, the psychic at the fair did tell me only one of my children would be psychic like me. It doesn't surprise me that it's my little River."

"He certainly is your twin. But enough about that. Back to your story before I burst. What were you going to tell me?"

"That my new friend Kalli can read minds," I blurted.

"Well, isn't that the cat's meow. Sounds like you four have a lot in common. I'm tickled pink you made some new friends. Just promise me you will be careful with a killer running around loose on board, and please leave the investigating to the authorities. You're precious cargo to me, you know."

"I know, Gran. Right back at you." I felt her smile through the line. "Love you. I'll update you when I know more." I hung up.

My grandmother and I had always been closer than my mother and me. But ever since I became a mother myself, my relationship with my own had gotten better. I was a daddy's girl all the way. My smile slipped a little. Speaking of daddies. I worried Mitch wouldn't be able to relate to River if he did turn out to be psychic like me. Mitch loved me unconditionally, and I knew he loved his son as well. But when it came to supernatural things, he had a hard time understanding, much less coping with them.

Maybe finding out River was showing signs of being psychic was the reason for my uneasiness. My stomach turned over and the hairs on the back of my neck prickled. I whipped around and searched the deck but didn't see anything amiss. Just passengers milling about, trying to salvage what they could of their vacation. I could have sworn I felt eyes on me just a moment ago.

But why?

What could I possibly have to do with Baron Von Wielig and what on earth could his killer possibly want with me?

"There you are." Mitch joined me by the rail, and I felt better already. "I've been looking all over for you."

"Here I am. I was just calling Granny and filling her in on the situation."

"How are the kids?"

"Loving life apparently. My parents and everyone else at the Inn are spoiling them rotten."

His chiseled face softened and the jagged scar beneath his whiskers pulsed once as he swallowed hard. "That's what families are for."

I cupped his cheek with my palm, knowing he was wishing his parents and sister were still around to spoil our children as well. "You're right. They are pretty special when they aren't driving me crazy."

He winked at me and turned his face into my palm to kiss it. "Let's get something to eat. I'm starving."

"Sounds good." I turned away from the rail and started to follow him when I ran straight into a man. He was average height, with a muscular frame, and a full head of gold and white hair. I recognized him immediately. "I'm so sorry, Mr. Overton."

"Please, call me Rafe."

"Only if you call me Sunny."

"Careful Sunny." He steadied me then let go, seeming a lot more comfortable than he had been this morning. "It took me until my fourth cruise to get my sea legs." He winked. "I wouldn't want you to fall overboard, too, now."

"Thanks." I puckered my brow as he walked away.

"Who was that?" Mitch kept his eyes on the man.

"Some art enthusiast I met earlier on the cruise excursion." I chewed my bottom lip, wondering if I was overthinking things like I usually did.

"Is anything wrong? You look puzzled."

"He said it took him until his fourth cruise to get his sea legs."

Mitch drew his eyebrows together. "What's so puzzling about that?"

"I saw him in Bermuda in the boutiques with Kalli." I looked Mitch in the eye. "He had just bought new rubber soled shoes because he said this was his first cruise."

"Well, now, that *is* a mystery, isn't it?" Mitch looked after the man until he disappeared below deck.

"It sure is." Just one more mystery I intended to solve.

~

Kalli

"I *told* you Isosceles no good! You no listen, Kalliope," Aunt Tasoula said, shouting into the phone by Ma. Ma called from our family's Greek restaurant, Aphrodite's, and put me on speaker phone. My family and Nik's were all there by the sound of it.

"How she supposed to listen, 'Soula?" Ma said. "Isosceles much bigger than a cruising ship. She no should have gone in the first place like her mama said. She no listen to *me*." I could hear Ma pat her chest. "You never listen to your mama, Kalli. And now look at what happened. You like a bobber on the ocean, ping ponging off the Devil's triangle. He playing with you. What's gonna happen when he decides to smash you to bits?"

"Ma, I told you. We're out of the triangle."

"You don't know for sure. What if Isosceles became Isosce-round? A giant circle who make you cruise round and round the merry-go-round. You get so dizzy you don't know which way is home. Poseidon no save you from the devil." I could just imagine her making the sign of the cross, and I fought hard not to roll my eyes. I loved my family, but sometimes their antics were even too much for me.

"This ship has a state-of-the-art navigation system, Ma. We're not in the Bermuda Triangle anymore. We're on course to go home."

"Then why you no move. Pop track you location on the mobile device, and he say you no move."

"Because of the murder. I'm sure you've seen the news."

"Oh, my Zeus! That was *your* cruising ship?" Aunt Tasoula screeched. "Oh, woe is me. Come on, Ophelia. I get the life jackets. You get the sunscreen. We go save our girl."

"Please tell me neither of you will try something crazy. Our ship is on lockdown. It's a crime scene and there is an investigation going on. No one is allowed to leave or come on board."

"We take—" my aunt started, her voice matter of fact, only the rest of her sentence was cut off.

I pressed my phone harder against my ear in time to hear Ma speaking.

"Tasoula, sometimes I no know where you head is at. We can't—" her voice crackled and faded in and out. "Maybe we—they no see—?" More noises filled the airwaves, and I wrinkled my nose in an attempt to decipher what she was talking about. "How hard can it be?" she finished with absolute clarity.

I shook my head. "Listen," I interrupted. "Nik and another detective we met are doing some investigating on their own. And the FBI has been called on board along with the ship's security detail. The captain is making sure they're taking every precaution to keep us all safe. Besides, I'm not alone. I made a friend. Her name is Sunshine, but everyone calls her Sunny. She's married to Detective Mitch Stone."

"Sunshine? Who names their daughter Sunshine?" Ma grunted.

"She told me she changed her name from Sylvia to Sunny." I wasn't very good at explaining things, and Ma was very protective of me. I didn't dare tell her I could read minds, and if I told her Sunny was psychic, there would be no stopping her from trying to come on board and rescue me.

"Aha." Ma raised her voice. "She no listen to *her* mama, either."

"I have a bad feeling those two gonna get in big trouble," Aunt Tasoula chimed in again. She should talk about getting into trouble. My aunt and my ma were the queens of finding trouble or being the cause of it.

"No one's going to get into trouble," I said calmly before I heard a loud pop and static once more crackled and whooshed in my ear. I climbed the stairs and headed up to the top deck where I spotted Sunny and Mitch talking to Nik. "Look, Ma, I have to go. I'm losing the signal. I'll keep you updated as I hear more. Give everyone my love."

"Wait, Kalli, I have an idea," Nik's ma, Chloe, said. "We can—"

And the line went dead.

I groaned, not wanting to even think about what the crazy Greek mamas were planning...or what they thought after we'd lost our connection. They probably thought Isosce-round had snapped together to form a straight line and squash me to bits...or an alien had abducted me.

Either way, it couldn't be good.

"There you are." Nik slipped his arm around me and kissed my cheek. "Look who I ran into. They were on their way to get some lunch at Seaside Savories and asked us to join them. Are you hungry?"

"I could eat. What's Seaside Savories?"

"The buffet." Nik watched me closely.

I smiled wide, trying to hide my distress, but Nik knew I was picky about the places I ate. Back home, I carried my own utensils, and I only ate in restaurants of people I knew who kept their kitchens spotless. Mostly, we ate at my parents' restaurant.

The thought of how many hands were on the buffet of a cruise ship this size terrified me.

So far the restaurants had agreed to let me take a tour of their kitchens, but I wanted to be flexible and try everything. I just hadn't counted on a buffet. For Nik, I was stepping out of my comfort zone by agreeing to this floating vessel of micro-organisms in the first place. I knew he wanted to eat with Mitch and Sunny.

"Who doesn't love a buffet?" Mitch asked with a wide smile. "So much food." He rubbed his stomach.

"Right." I swallowed hard. "So much food. What more could anyone ask for?" I tried for a smile.

"Great." Nik kept his arm around me as we followed Mitch and Sunny. *Thank you, Ballas. I know that wasn't easy. This means a lot.*

I reached up and threaded my fingers through his, giving his hand a little squeeze. Inhaling a deep breath, I held it a few beats, then let it out slowly. I could do this. As we entered the large room surrounded by windows with the same buffet on each side, we passed soups and crackers, salad and toppings, sandwiches and chips, hot dishes, cold dishes, side dishes, grilled meats, pizzas, and any kind of dessert you could think of.

My insides churned over how it was possible to keep all the cold, room temperature, and hot items at the perfect temperature so bacteria didn't grow, let alone how to enforce making people use the tongs and the germs inevitably left behind on said tongs. I visibly gagged, however, one look at Nik's face made it all worthwhile.

We found a table, and the men took off to fill their plates with the eagerness of two Grizzly bears in a stream during a salmon run. Sunny touched my arm. *Sit tight. I'll be right back.* Then she walked off, stopped and waited for a moment until a woman emerged from a side door behind the buffet. She said something to her, and then the woman disappeared once more, returning shortly and handing her a tray. Sunny smiled at the woman and nodded then returned to our table with a huge grin on her face.

"What is that?" I asked, staring at a tray full of carefully wrapped sandwiches, pieces of whole unpeeled fruit, and small individual bags of chips plus two wrapped cookies.

"Our lunch." Sunny winked.

"But how did you know?"

She tapped her temple. "I'm psychic, remember?" She giggled. "I met Ursula yesterday and did a reading for her, then had a vision of us at lunch today. So, I made a request as a favor and gave her careful instructions on sanitation and what to make." Sunny spread her hands to the trays in front of us in grand fashion. "Voila, lunch."

My eyes grew misty. What a sweet gesture from a woman I barely knew, yet I felt like I had known her forever. "I don't know what to say. Thank you so much."

"Of course." She reached out and touched my arm, and I didn't squirm once. *That's what friends are for.*

"Special friends," I said, and then we both took off our wrappers and dug in.

Mitch and Nik returned with heaping plates, and Nik's eyes grew huge when he saw me eating my lunch. His eyebrow arched high.

"Did you try the sandwich table?" I took a big bite of mine, chewing and swallowing without wincing even once. "The food's great."

His mouth parted as he gaped at me, and Sunny shot me a wink from behind him. "I'll keep that in mind for next time," he finally replied after he found his voice.

Mitch looked between the two of us and blinked, then shrugged and sat down at the table. The men ate in silence in between moans of appreciation.

"So, I was thinking we could talk to the Dubois first," Nik said. "Milton didn't seem too fond of Baron."

"Good idea," Mitch agreed. "I got the same impression."

"We heard Simon kicked Baron off an excursion after he littered on the island." I wrinkled my nose in distaste. "We ran into him in the boutique."

"Milton and Mavis were there, and Milton wasn't too happy. He left the store without buying a thing." Sunny hoisted one shoulder. "I could use my ability to see if Mavis knows anything. I promised her a reading, after all."

"That's a great idea." I nodded. "And I can read her mind while you're doing the reading to see if she's being truthful."

"I don't think that's a good idea for either of you." Mitch looked at me and then turned to Sunny. "You're a mother now. Think of the children."

"I *am* thinking of the children and solving this case quicker so we can get home to them. Besides, you're a father now, too." Sunny frowned, crossing her arms over her chest. "I assist the police department as a consultant back home all the time."

"You might assist, Tink, but let's face the facts." Mitch leaned back and smoothed a hand down his polo shirt, giving a satisfied pat when he reached his stomach. "You're not a *real* cop like Detective Stevens and me."

"Yeah, Detective Stone is right, honey." Nik looked at me pensively as he adjusted the waistband of his cargo shorts after the mountain of food he'd inhaled. "We're talking murder on a cruise ship. This case is way out of your league. I think it's best if you leave the investigating to the professionals."

"Last I checked, small town detectives don't meet the requirements of investigating murder at high seas, either." I crossed my arms over my chest as well. "All cruise ships are required by international law to carry a Belgian ex-chief of police turned private investigator to handle that sort of thing. And most likely they will call in the FBI since we're the closest to US soil."

"Well, we're closer to the real deal than either of you are. And last *I* checked there was no crime in talking to people." Nik shrugged.

"Exactly." Mitch nodded.

"But I—" I started to say.

"I agree, too," Sunny blurted as she touched my arm. "It's settled then. You detectives go do your thing." *Let them go, I have a plan.*

"Yes, go on with you then. I'm sure Sunny and I can find something to do."

Mitch and Nik eyed each other.

"Remember, there's a killer on the loose. Don't do anything stupid, Tink. I don't need any more gray hairs."

"Me?" Sunny's hand fluttered to her chest. "Don't be silly, Grumpy Pants. We'll just find some fun extracurricular activities to partake in."

"That's what I'm afraid of."

5

SUNNY

"Where are we going?" Kalli asked as we left the buffet.

"To check out the murder victim's body." I headed for the elevators. "The captain said they found evidence that indicated Baron was murdered and didn't jump off the ship on his own. I want to see for myself what the evidence is."

"Too bad I can't read his mind."

"He hasn't been dead that long." I looked around to make sure we were alone. "I might be able to pick up a reading from his body."

"Ew, I don't like to be touched to begin with, but I draw the line at touching a corpse." Kalli shuddered.

I shrugged as we stepped into an elevator. "It's not that bad."

"Rigor mortis, or postmortem rigidity, is the fourth stage of death characterized by the stiffening of a corpse's limbs. That freaks me out. Chemical changes in the muscles are what causes this postmortem."

"Interesting."

"Did you know that in humans, rigor mortis can occur as early as four hours after a person dies?"

"I did not know that."

"He probably won't be stiff anymore, though. Rigor mortis is not permanent and begins to pass within hours of onset. Typically, it lasts no longer than eight hours when a body has been at room temperature. First, they had to bring him back on board, and then the doctor had to examine him and pronounce him dead before he could be transferred to the morgue. Rigor mortis has most likely passed. He's probably still not in refrigeration yet, either, because of the ongoing investigation."

I blinked. "And you know all of this how?"

Kalli shrugged. "After the death of my biological mother and her missing corpse, I did a deep dive into what the human body goes through postmortem."

"Okay, that's a story you need to finish telling me sometime. For now, we're headed to the morgue while the body is still available." I kept walking with purpose. We only had so long before our men would come looking for us.

"Morgues freak me out, too, but at least the morgue will be cold, so that's good." Kalli seemed to be on the same wavelength that I was, judging by her hurried strides.

"I hate the cold." I shivered. "How is that a good thing?"

"Fewer germs." Kalli slathered her hands with her ever-ready bottle of hand sanitizer as we rode the rest of the way in silence until the elevator door opened on the lowest deck accessible to passengers.

Right after we found out a murder had happened, I had asked the medical examiner where they were keeping the body. I pretended to be disturbed about the idea of seeing a dead body. She had assured me they had medical facilities with doctors and nurses for sick or injured *living* passengers located on various decks near common areas like the main atrium for convenience, but not to worry. They had a morgue and infirmary for the medical examiner to examine and store the body of the deceased on a lower deck for the crew, which wasn't accessible to passengers.

"The morgue is on *this* floor?" Kalli blinked.

"No, but we need a disguise." It was a lower floor with a laundry room for the crew. I waited until a woman who was around our size who had on a room steward uniform left. "Let's go."

I gestured to Kalli to follow me. We slipped into the room and quickly located the right dryer with the type of uniforms we needed. We slipped the clothes on over our own shorts and t-shirts and then quickly left the room.

"What do we do now," Kalli whispered.

"Find the crew elevators and take them to the lower decks until we find the morgue." I nodded to other crew members as we passed them. It was a large ship. We got a few odd looks from the other room stewards, but the rest of the staff working in other departments wouldn't have a clue if we belonged or not.

"Hey, look." Kalli tapped my arm and pointed to a man with a stack of lab coats who entered the elevator.

We waited a beat and then pressed the button. The elevator came up from the fourth floor. That had to be the floor where the morgue was located. The doors opened and the elevator was empty, so we hopped in. It didn't stop at any other floors until the fourth floor. We exited, and I breathed a sigh of relief that the floor also contained crew quarters. At least we would have a reason to be there if we pretended to be on our way to our room.

I pulled Kalli into a doorway and held her arm.

*Look, the guy with the lab coats just came out of that room.
That has to be the morgue.*

She nodded silently, and we waited until he rode the elevator back up. This was our chance. We slipped into the dimly lit morgue and silently entered the examination room. The smell of antiseptics, formaldehyde, and other medical smells hit me hard.

I hated hospitals, especially morgues.

"I can sense a strong presence here." I grabbed my throat, feeling uncomfortable. Like it was difficult to breathe. The sensation of being suffocated hit me hard, and I inhaled as deeply as I could. "It's almost overwhelming."

"Focus, Sunny. Please. We're here to find evidence that will solve this case so we can get off this death trap."

"Right, sorry." I snapped out of it. "Let's get to work."

We approached the table where the body lay covered by a white sheet. Kalli covered her mouth and nose with her hand. I removed the sheet and felt sucker punched for a moment. No matter how many dead bodies I saw, it never got any easier, especially when it was someone I had met. Blowing out a heap of air, I focused and studied his body. He had marks on his neck and arms, indicating signs of a struggle.

Kalli gasped. "Look at these marks, Sunny. It seems like Baron fought back. I mean, he wasn't a big guy like our men. He was an average sized man, but still. Someone had to be strong enough to do this to him."

"Or desperate enough. You would be surprised the strength someone can muster when adrenaline gets pumping." I placed my hand on Baron's cold forehead. "I'll try to connect with his spirit and see if it can give us any clues."

Closing my eyes, I regulated my breathing and concentrated. My mind's eye narrowed into tunnel vision just like it always did when I had a vision. I was suddenly in Baron's body. We were standing in a dark corner of the ship, arguing and struggling. I broke free and climbed the ladder to a lifeboat to try to escape my attacker and slid open the door to the cover.

My attacker was right behind me, and we tumbled inside.

When my attacker wrapped their hands around my neck, I couldn't breathe. I clawed at the hands to no avail. I couldn't go out this way. I had so much I needed to fix first. It wasn't fair to her. She was all I had, and she would never know how much I loved her. The world around me was fading, and the last of my strength left me.

Then suddenly the hands let go. I felt someone pull me out of the lifeboat. Maybe there was a chance I would make it after all? Then the hands let go of me, and I was weightless. The sensation of falling, falling, falling backward filled me with fear until I hit the water hard and felt a snap in my neck.

Then there was nothing.

"Sunny, are you okay?" Kalli's voice broke through my gasps for air, and I was snapped back to the present.

I wiped the streaming tears from my eyes as Kalli stared at me with concern. "I felt shock, then fear, and finally panic."

"Does this happen to you every time you have a vision?" She frowned.

"Yes, it's like I become the person. Whatever they feel at that moment in time is what I feel. I relive it."

"That's horrible."

"It can be. But it can also be beautiful. That's why I keep doing it."

"Better you than me. I don't always like hearing people's thoughts, but at least I don't have to feel their emotions. Did you see anything else?"

I squinted, concentrating. "It was dark, but there was a struggle. Then a lifeboat. And finally falling into the cold, dark sea. Baron was strangled, but he didn't die from that. He was pushed, and the fall caused him to break his neck when he hit the water.

"Oh, wow. That's awful." She shook her head. "Did he defend himself before he was pushed?"

"Yes, actually." I closed my eyes for a moment, remembering, and then looked at Kalli as I spoke. "He scratched at his attacker's hands."

"Good." She nodded. "We need to look for someone with marks on their hands."

"Agreed." I carefully covered Baron's body back up with the sheet. "When he knew he was losing, he thought something strange."

"Like what?"

"He wanted to fix things. He thought it wasn't fair to her, and that she would never know how much he loved her."

"Wow." Kalli's eyes widened. "I thought he was a ladies' man. Maybe he wasn't after all. Did you have any insight into who the woman might be?"

"No...but I know where we can start."

She puckered her brow. "Where's that?"

"We need to check out that lifeboat."

"Which one?"

I paused and bit my lip. "That's the kicker. I'm not sure. I just know it was dark and shadowed. I think I might be able to recognize it if I saw it."

She looked doubtful. "Do you know how many

lifeboats there are? This ship is huge. That will take forever to find the right one."

I held my hands up. "Then I guess we'd better get started. We need to find more evidence to back up our conclusions."

Kalli groaned. "I have a feeling I'm not going to like this investigation."

Suddenly, the sound of footsteps outside the examination room startled us.

"Someone's coming! Quick, hide!" I looked around, but there was only one small cabinet. "I'm the smaller of the two of us, so I'll squeeze behind that."

"Where am I supposed to hide?"

There was only one other choice. I yanked one of the six refrigeration units open. "You said you liked the cold."

Kalli's eyes grew huge, and she gaped at me. "Uh, uh, no way. I can't do that. I'm claustrophobic."

Noises grew closer with voices right outside the door.

"I would switch places with you, but you won't fit behind here, and you'll need me to let you out." I shushed her and pointed my finger at the unit as the noises became louder.

You owe me, she mouthed as I helped stuff her into the unit. She started to change her mind and poke her head out, so I mouthed, *sorry*, and closed the door, giving me just enough time to slip behind the cabinet.

"Security," an older man's voice said. "Anyone in here? I heard a noise."

Silence.

"You're just being paranoid, Roger," said a younger man's voice. "There's Doc down the hall. She's headed our way now."

The security guard grumbled something about

being an empath and feeling the energy of a larger-than-life spirit and the ship being haunted. He told the spirit to go away and vowed to sage his room again as he left the morgue, closing the door behind him.

I waited a beat during the silence to make sure they both had left and then peeked into the empty room before I slid out from behind the cabinet as quickly as I could and opened the door to the refrigerator. Kalli's lips were blue. She scrambled out, no need for my help on her exit. "Th-That was traumatizing."

"I know. I'm so sorry." I closed the refrigerator door.

"I-I'm beyond cold," she whispered with chattering teeth, "and we were way too close to getting caught. You owe me. I will never be the same again."

"Next time, you make the plan. I'll do whatever you want. Promise. But for now, let's get out of here," I said and peeked out the door.

Way down the hall, Doctor Bella Chopra was talking to the security guards. Kalli and I slipped out and headed in the other direction before she saw us. As quickly as we could, we made our way to the elevator and back up to the passenger floors. Ditching our uniforms in the trash of a bathroom, we entered the atrium and ran smack dab into Mitch and Nik.

"Where have you two been? We've been looking everywhere." Mitch narrowed his eyes. "What trouble did you get into this time, Tink?"

"I have no idea what you're talking about." I adjusted my wrinkled clothes.

"We went to the spa," Kalli jumped in, her teeth no longer chattering but her face still pale.

"You hate the spa," Nik added suspiciously.

"They had a new cold therapy treatment that didn't involve being touched, and no germs." She shrugged, then wrapped her arms around her middle. "At least I tried something new like I promised you I would."

He looked impressed, eyeing her up and down. "I'm proud of you, Ballas. Maybe we can go together next time."

"That would be a hard no, Detective." Kalli shuddered. "One round of cold therapy was more than enough for me. Enough of the interrogation into our whereabouts. What I want to know is where the two of you were."

Nik gave Mitch a funny look.

Mitch just shook his head. "Let's just say the Dubois are very interesting people."

"What do you mean?" I asked.

"It turns out this isn't the first time that Mavis and Milton have been on a cruise where a passenger died." Nik rubbed his hands together. "The plot thickens."

"You're kidding?" I asked in shock.

"Yeah, isn't murder at high seas uncommon?" Kalli speculated.

"One would think." Mitch pulled out his favorite notebook and flipped through his notes.

I had to chuckle. Even on vacation he had a hard time turning work off. It didn't surprise me that he'd snuck his little notebook into his suitcase as if he were anticipating, or *hoping*, he might have to investigate something. But who was I to judge? I had snuck a few crystals, essential oils, and some sage into my suitcase as well just in case someone might need my *assistance*.

"About five years ago, they went on a cruise with a group of wealthy friends from their social circle when one of them died of food poisoning," Mitch continued. "Foul play was suspected, but they never did catch the killer."

"Makes me wonder about the couple." Nik looked pensive. "Two wealthy people were murdered, and the common denominator are the Dubois."

"Same. Apparently, Milton didn't like that guy, either." Mitch raised a brow.

"Well, there's one way to find out if they were involved," I said.

"There is?" Kalli asked.

"I never did give Mavis that reading I promised her."

"I don't think you going off alone with either of them is such a good idea, Sunny." Mitch frowned, the worry lines between his brows sinking deeper.

"I won't be alone."

"That's right," Kalli looped her arm through mine, "because she'll have me."

"And we'll choose a public location," I added. "Like The Library. I saw this quant lounge that had drinks and books and cozy nooks. It will be the perfect place to get Mavis to relax and open up."

"That's not a bad idea." Nik shrugged. "For amateurs, that is."

Kalli narrowed her eyes. "These amateurs are going to beat you at your own game and solve this case first, Detective. Let the games begin."

"Game on, Ballas."

6

KALLI

The Library was my kind of lounge. A rich, mahogany bar ran along the far wall. The rest of the walls were lined with books, and the room was filled with cozy chairs and couches with end tables and lamps.

A hot cup of tea and a good book was my idea of a lovely afternoon.

Sunny seemed to read *my* mind this time. "You grab the table. I'll get the tea." She headed to the bar where Frankie and Courtney were waiting on customers. Mystery Girl was at the end, with her head bent close to Frankie's.

I picked a table in the corner where we could see anyone who walked in, yet our privacy could be maintained. Sunny smiled as she made her way back over to join me.

"I thought Frankie and Courtney worked at the Sky Deck bar?" I asked.

"I asked him the same thing. He said all the bartenders and cocktails waitresses rotate between bars, depending on the time of day." Sunny shrugged. "Courtney said she would bring the pot of tea over when it's done. I ordered some biscuits as well. I met the baker. Her kitchen is immaculate." Sunny winked.

"Sounds wonderful." I smiled my appreciation. "Mystery Girl gets around as much as Baron did. She looks pretty chummy with Frankie."

"He introduced us. Her name is Gracie. She didn't say much else. She looked like she had been crying. Lance probably dumped her same as he did Natalia." Sunny winced. "I didn't want to pry, so I left them to their conversation. You know how it is with bartenders. They're like therapists."

"Very true." I looked toward the empty lounge door, wondering if something had happened. "So have you heard from Mavis?"

Sunny checked her watch. "She should have been here by now. I wonder what's keeping her?"

"So, how do these readings work? Is it like the vision you had for Baron?"

"Sometimes I get pulled into a vision, but many times, I simply interpret the images I see. Back home, I use fortune telling tools to help with my readings. Since I promised I wouldn't work on this cruise, I didn't bring anything but my crystals and oils with me. I did, however, ask Mavis to bring along a personal item. Something that has meaning to her that she wears or uses often. Maybe that's what's holding her up?"

"There she is now." I pointed at the entrance to the lounge.

Mavis walked in and looked around. When she spotted us, she waved and hurried over to sit down. She was a little red-faced and out of breath.

"Sorry I'm tardy. I couldn't get Milton away from the poker table, and he needed to take his pills. I left him in our cabin and hurried here as quickly as I could. Hope you haven't been waiting for long?"

"No worries," Sunny said and patted the empty chair beside her. "We ordered tea and biscuits."

"Well, isn't that just lovely." Mavis sat and placed her large tote bag on the floor beside her.

"Here you are, ladies." Courtney set the steaming pot of tea in the middle of the table and a tray of delicious looking biscuits on fancy plates with dainty teacups next to them.

"Thank you so much, dear." Mavis patted her hand then looked over at the bar and wiggled her fingers in a wave. Frankie blew her a kiss, and her cheeks grew even more flushed. "You tell that handsome young man I'll see him later for something a bit stronger. He makes a mean martini with a side of stimulating conversation." Laughter bubbled out of her mouth as if she were twenty years younger.

"Will do," Courtney said then mumbled as she walked away, "That man has no shame. Anything for a tip."

"So, are you ready to get started?" Sunny poured the tea and handed us each a cup while I passed out the biscuits.

I discreetly ran my napkin around the rim of my cup three times and snapped open my handy straw before taking a sip, then I nibbled on a biscuit. *Delicious.* I looked at Mavis curiously as she rummaged through her humongous bag.

"Here we go." She pulled out a gorgeous double-layered diamond flower brooch with a pearl in the center. "This has been in my family for two centuries."

"Aren't you worried about having it on this cruise?" I asked. "Nik's ma always wore a necklace that was a family heirloom. She had no idea how much it was worth until it got stolen. Thank goodness she got it back. It's now under lock and key."

"Oh, I know exactly how much my brooch is worth, and that's the point. I wear it everywhere. It's my good luck charm. What's the purpose of having nice things if you can never show them off?" Mavis handed the brooch to Sunny.

"Thank you. It's lovely. I'm going to close my eyes while I hold it and see if anything comes through."

"This is so exciting." Mavis clapped her hands.

Sunny took deep slow breaths while holding the brooch in her hand. Her eyes were closed, and she looked like she was concentrating. A slight smile tipped up the corners of her lips. "You certainly have had a lot of fun with this brooch. Cruises, all-inclusive resorts, international trips...you've taken so many, especially recently."

"We do love to travel."

Sunny's forehead wrinkled. "I don't see you traveling in the near future. That's not to say you won't at some time." She paused a moment. "I'm not sure who this is. A petite woman with a large hat and red hair is coming through, insisting I pass along a message."

"Oh, my word. That has to be my great grand-mother. The brooch you're holding was hers, then my grandmother's, then my mother's and now mine. I'm named after her. She died when I was still a child, but I remember her. She had a huge collection of hats and the most magnificent red hair. My hair was the same shade before it turned snow white." Mavis ran a hand over her chic style.

"Well, your great-grandmother is determined to warn you to pay attention to the people around you. It's not clear who she's talking about, but it's going to happen soon. Someone will need to see a doctor, but they will need convincing to go. It's important for the person to listen to the doctor's advice."

Mavis's hand fluttered to her chest. "Well, that's alarming. Who is it?"

"It's not clear. Just know she insists you take any health-related crisis you come across seriously, including your own."

"Oh, my." Her face paled. "Okay, I will. Is there anything else?"

Sunny concentrated harder then she sucked in a sharp breath, and her eyes flew open and stared into her hand.

"What is it?" I asked.

Sunny's gaze looked troubled as she glanced at me, then focused back on Mavis. "Trust your gut. Deep down you know the truth."

"Whatever are you referring to?"

"This isn't your great-grandmother's brooch." Sunny handed the piece of jewelry to Mavis. "It's a fake."

"That's not possible. It never leaves my sight. You must be mistaken, dear." Mavis glanced at her watch. "Oh, my. Look at the time. I must be going. Milton will be waiting for me."

"Here, let me help you." I stood and picked up her tote bag, not letting go when her hand touched mine. *I'm sorry, Great- Grandma. I hope you can forgive me.*

"Thank you, dear. I've got it from here." Mavis looked at me strangely when I still held onto her bag.

"Sorry." I let go.

Mavis headed for the door.

"I think she's upset over the brooch being a fake." Sunny looked at me.

"I think she's upset because she *knew* it was a fake." I looked at Sunny.

Her eyes widened. "She knew it was a fake? How?"

I shrugged and then we heard a commotion. Looking over by the door, I couldn't believe my eyes. Mavis Dubois had collapsed and was lying motionless by the doorway.

~

Sunny

"Kalli, meet me on deck seven on the walkway outside," I said into my phone through the cruise app. After Mavis came to, Kalli and I convinced her to let the doctor look at her, reminding her of her reading. I was pretty sure her collapse was caused by more than a fainting spell. Once we knew she was in good hands, we split up to join our men and fill them in on what had happened.

"What's on deck seven?" Kalli pulled me from my thoughts.

"You'll see."

"Starboard or port, forward or aft?"

"Ummm...excuse me?" I said into my cell phone.

"Sorry. The port side is the left, with the right side being the starboard. And the forward or bow is the front with the aft being the back. So where are you?"

"Port and aft, I guess." I chuckled. Kalli knew a mountain of facts about all sorts of things. She would make an amazing trivia partner. "Hurry up, sailor."

"Aye aye, Captain. I'll be right there." She laughed and hung up.

I was happy she had finally started to relax a little. I stood outside on deck seven, waiting for her at the back of the boat. I looked around, but this area of the ship was deserted. There were no windows from restaurants and people who liked to walk or run the outside of the ship tended to do that on the upper deck by the pool. I had walked every section of the ship that contained the lifeboats until a *feeling* came over me, telling me I was in the right place.

"There you are." She came to a stop by my side. "I told the guys I was meeting you for a walk."

"Good. The last thing I need is for Mitch to worry even more about me." I shook my head. "I told him about the reading for Mavis and about her fainting. He was headed to check on Mavis when I left."

"Nik and I passed him talking to Milton when you called, so I told them I was meeting you to go for a walk. Nik was meeting Maria because she asked him to accompany her to the casino to play blackjack in her late husband's honor. Since the doctor was keeping Mavis for observation, Milton and Mitch decided to join Nik and Maria. So, we have time to roam with them being distracted."

"Roam no further." I pointed up to a large lifeboat raised above us that was secured alongside of the deck out of the way.

In the case of an emergency, the ship's crew would climb the ladder to the platform up top, release the boat, then use the mechanical davit to slowly lower the covered boat full of supplies to the deck for loading. Once the passengers were on board, the machine would finish safely lowering the boat to the ocean.

"Are you sure this is the right one?" Kalli looked up, studying the vessel.

"Oh, I'm sure. I *felt* it." I rubbed my hands together. "Follow me." I started to climb the ladder to the top of the lifeboat.

"Hey, wait a minute. I thought I was supposed to

make the next plan after you locked me in that ice box," Kalli pointed out from close behind me.

"No time to waste." I climbed higher. "No one knows he was up here but us, so there might still be a clue to find."

"I don't know how I let you talk me into these things," I heard her mumble as the ladder shook beneath me.

When I reached the top, I stepped onto the platform. There was a door on the side of the lifeboat cover, just like the one from my vision. I slid it up and climbed inside. Kalli quickly followed.

"Should I close it behind us?" she asked.

"No, we won't be able to see anything very well if you do. Besides, unless someone climbs up the ladder to the platform, they won't be able to see the open door from down below."

"Good point. What are we looking for?"

"I'm not sure. All I know is that Baron and his killer were in here. I think the killer thought they strangled him and had to get rid of the body. So, they pulled him out and pushed him over the side."

We started searching all around the large interior of the lifeboat. There were emergency supplies and boxes of high caloric biscuits for a week's worth of food per person. Ropes, flares, first aid containers, thermal blankets, and more. I was about to say let's go when a flash caught my eye. I bent down and looked beneath a bench.

"What is it?" Kalli asked.

"A watch." I squinted. "That looks like the time piece Baron was showing off that first night at dinner. I wonder if the killer was after this."

Kalli looked pensive. "Or maybe it just fell off."

"Maybe, but either way, maybe we can pull a print

off it." Using the edge of my skirt, I picked up the watch and slipped it into my pocket.

"We should tell someone so they can dust this lifeboat." Kalli nodded once. "It's the right thing to do."

I raised a brow at her. "And how exactly would we explain how we know Baron was in here?"

Suddenly, the lifeboat shook like someone was climbing the ladder. Before we could react, the door slid closed, rocking the boat. What light was left of the day streamed in through the small windows.

I ran over and tried to open the door. "It's stuck." I tapped on it several times. "Hello? Is anyone out there?"

Silence.

Kalli grabbed a life jacket and put it on. "I don't like this one bit. What if we fall? Oh, this is so bad."

"That won't happen. We're secured to the davit which lowers us slowly to avoid sudden falls and injuries."

The boat shifted, and we felt someone working outside the door.

"Hey, let us out!" I shouted.

They ignored us and kept doing something.

"Oh, God, what if it's the killer. We should call the guys," Kalli said.

"No time." I shoved a life jacket at her. "Put this on and hold on tight."

"Why?" she did as I instructed.

"I think we're about to—"

We both screamed for all we were worth as the lifeboat rolled and fell to the ocean with a heavy splash. We were thrown about, bouncing off various items. Finally, we settled and just rocked up and down.

"That was terrifying. Are you okay?" Kalli asked.

"Just a few bumps and bruises," I replied, my heartbeat thundering in my ears. "How about you?"

"Same." She scrambled over to a window and looked out. "The current is carrying us away from the anchored ship. What do we do?"

I whipped out my phone and tried to call Mitch, but the app only worked on board. And the cell service inside this capsule wouldn't be good. I frowned as I felt a cold, wet sensation and looked down. "How is there water coming in?" I stared at the quickly growing puddle of water at my feet. "The killer must have tampered with it. Can you swim?"

"In the dirty ocean?" Her eyes grew huge. "With sharks and whales and...sharks? Shark attacks are growing more common every day with global warming. I knew I shouldn't have eaten tuna fish for lunch."

"We're not going to be shark bait. But honestly, I'd rather that than going down with the boat, locked in a watery tomb." I shuddered, thinking of what we could do.

"How are we going to get out of here?" Kalli's voice climbed several octaves. "No one was supposed to see us. They must have followed us. Sunny, we need to open this door before we drown!"

"Wait, I remember seeing something that might help." I waded through the now ankle-deep water. "We need to stay calm. Everything will be okay."

It was during times like these when my immortal cat, Morty, would appear from out of nowhere and save the day. What I wouldn't give for that sassy cat right now. But with oceans between us, I'd have to be resourceful.

I opened one of the cabinets I had looked through and found a flare, holding it proudly in front of Kalli.

"How is that thing going to open this door?" She pushed hard against it, and I saw the wood give a little.

"Kalli, yes! Let's work together and force it open." We pushed with all our might, but the wood didn't break. It did separate enough where I could see part of the latch which kept us prisoner. "Ugh, we need to find something that will fit between the crack and flip the latch open."

"Like what? I can barely see in here. For Zeus's sake, there's everything *but* tools in here." I watched in awe as she dug through her purse, which was stuffed to the zipper, to pull out her cell phone to shine a light.

"Kalli, your bag."

"What about it?" she looked down and shrugged.

"I think I saw something long." I waded over to her, excitement filling me with hope. "Was it a nail file?"

"I have a nail file, but it's not long enough. Maybe you saw my comb. Aunt Tasoula sent it with me to help tease my hair in this humidity." Kalli pulled out a comb with wide teeth and a long, thin handle that came to a slight point at the end.

"I think that will work!" I snatched it out of her hand and returned to the door. "You push the door, and I'll stick the end of the comb through and flip the latch."

It took a couple tries before the latch finally opened. Sliding the door up, we were hit by a wave smacking the side of the boat and nearly fell out. Not wasting another second, I shot the flare high in the air. A few moments later, a horn sounded from the ship, and we looked at each other in relief.

They saw us and would send help.

"Come on. We need to get to higher ground." I led

the way outside, and we climbed on the roof of the lifeboat and then tightened our life jackets.

The waves were rolling high with the strong wind, and the boat started to sink quicker.

"If my ma and my aunt could see me now, they would have fits for sure." Kalli wrung her hands as her feet dipped beneath the surface.

"Look, I see a boat headed toward us." I pointed, relief surging through me. "We might have to swim for it." I looked at a pale Kalli. "This boat is sinking quickly, and we don't want to get pulled under with it."

"I was afraid you were going to say that." She pulled off her belt. "Here, let me loop it through our life jackets so we don't lose each other."

"Good idea." I stood still while she fastened it. "Okay, you ready?"

"No, but we don't have another choice."

We held hands, counted to three, and jumped. The water was so cold. We started kicking towards the boat coming at us. I glanced over my shoulder and couldn't believe how fast the lifeboat sank. Our life jackets had beacons that flashed once we hit the water. We waved and shouted as the rescue boat drew closer.

Finally, the boat pulled up beside us. A man in a security uniform reached over the edge and helped us up inside the boat. The other officers quickly gave us each a thermal blanket to wrap up in to prevent hypothermia. The water in the Atlantic Ocean this close to the United States was still cold this time of year.

"I'm Chief Security Officer Justin Cho, and you are?" He had a jet-black buzz cut and intense dark eyes.

"Sunny Stone." My lips shivered.

"Kalli Ballas." Her teeth chattered.

"We can explain," I said.

He looked us both in the eye. "Good, because the captain wants to see you both in her office as soon as medical clears you."

"Can someone call my husband?"

"And my boyfriend?"

"They're already with the captain."

"Oh boy." Kalli groaned.

I blinked. "What does that mean?"

"That you're all in a lot of trouble."

7

KALLI

"The last time I checked, none of you were Agatha Christie or Sherlock Holmes," Captain Heather Hughes said as we entered the bridge. She was a tall, lean woman with icy blue eyes, short silver hair slicked back, a no-nonsense expression on her face, and a tone that brooked no argument.

Clearly, she was not amused.

She stood with her arms and ankles crossed, leaning back against the desk in her office. The walls and door were glass that overlooked a counter full of instruments on the bridge, with a long row of windows looking over the front of the ship so she could keep an eye on the navigation.

She wore a short sleeve white button-down shirt with a patch on each shoulder that contained four gold bars. Her shirt was tucked into white dress pants worn over black dress shoes. And a white hat with a black brim and gold badge in the center. The officers beside her were dressed the same but with fewer bars, depending on their rank. This is how they dressed every day, except on formal nights for the captain's dinner. Then they wore black dress uniforms.

"In our defense, we at least are *real* detectives." Nik gestured to himself and Mitch, "unlike some people I could mention." He didn't look at me.

He didn't dare.

"Yeah, we were just lending our services to help expedite the investigation." Mitch stood tall.

"Is that what you call it." The captain looked at them both and then pushed a button on a remote.

A video started playing on a large screen of multiple camera images. Nik and Mitch in the casino, dividing, distracting, and questioning various guests. Nik and Mitch in several bars, buying rounds and taking notes. Nik and Mitch in the cigar lounge, passing out stogies, not leaving passengers alone. Nik and Mitch tailing passengers and spying on them.

"We don't need your help, Detectives," an equally tall woman said.

"Seems to me you can use all the help you can get to question over thirty-eight hundred passengers, Officer...?" Mitch raised a brow at the fiery redhead.

"FBI Special Agent Amy Randolph." The woman flashed her badge. "Captain Hughes has her security team, with Chief Officer Justin Cho at the helm, as well as me. We've got things covered here."

"Not to mention all cruise ships are required by international law to carry a Belgian ex chief of police turned private investigator to handle murder at high seas."

"See, I told you so," I said to Nik and Mitch, then I looked at the captain. "I knew that." I patted my chest and grinned.

The captain did not.

I wiped the grin off my face and remained silent as she continued.

She pointed to a buff bald man with a square jaw. "Meet Edgarton Maes, better known as Eddie."

Eddie nodded once.

"Too many cooks in the kitchen doesn't work for anyone, gentleman." Captain Hughes gave them a no-nonsense look. "I suggest you both worry about yourselves and stop interfering, or I'll have to lock you up in the brig."

"Lock *us* up?" Nik's jaw fell open. "What about them?" He thrust his finger in our direction.

I glared.

"They are most definitely a danger to themselves," Mitch added.

Sunny gasped.

"Don't even get me started." The captain turned on more video footage.

Sunny bit her bottom lip.

I cringed.

We'd totally forgotten about the security cameras.

I tried not to groan of embarrassment as images of us riding the crew elevator down and then sneaking into the laundry room to borrow steward uniforms. Mitch grunted over that one, shaking his head. Then more videos of us sneaking into the morgue. Sunny's vision, then her shoving me into a refrigeration unit. I shuddered over the memory.

Nik gaped at me, but I refused to look at him.

More videos played out before us. Sunny and I reaching the lifeboat, but the area was shadowed. You couldn't see us climb up. All you saw was the boat rolling off its platform and falling down to the ocean with a big splash. And then the last video of a soaked Sunny and me climbing out of a rescue boat and back onto the cruise ship.

"We can explain," Sunny said.

"Please, enlighten me, ladies." Captain Hughes eyed us curiously.

"You see, I'm psychic. When you announced Baron's death wasn't a suicide or accident and there was evidence of foul play, I knew I had to see the body. I was hoping I could still pull a reading from it, and I did."

"I'm all ears." She looked skeptical.

"Just as I suspected, the marks on his neck indicated he was strangled. When I touched him, I had a vision. Baron was running from the killer when he climbed the lifeboat ladder. This particular lifeboat is in the shadows and blocked from the cameras. The killer followed, but I couldn't see who it was in my vision. They struggled inside the lifeboat. After the killer choked Baron, they obviously thought he was dead. So, they dragged his body out of the lifeboat and pushed him over the edge to get rid of the evidence. Baron died by snapping his neck when he hit the water."

"So you're telling us that's why you climbed into the lifeboat." Agent Amy studied the tapes more closely.

"Exactly," I said. "We went to look for a clue."

"And did you find any clues?" PI Eddie flipped open a notebook.

"I found this." Sunny pulled out Baron's watch from her skirt pocket.

"For all I know, you two could have killed Baron and gone back for his watch." Eddie eyed the watch closely. "That looks like an expensive time piece."

"Well, we certainly didn't push ourselves into the ocean," I said. "Someone followed us and latched the door closed behind us. They must have released the boat and unhooked it from the lowering mechanism because we hit the water hard enough to put a crack in the boat. Or the person tampered with it before releasing us. It had to be the killer."

"I was hoping you could get a print, but now, after I swam in the ocean with it, it might be compromised." Sunny handed the watch to Amy. "Also, Baron said something about if he died it wouldn't be fair to some woman, and that she would never know how much he loved her. I have no idea who the woman is."

"Is that all?"

Sunny looked pensive then said firmly, "Yes."

"That's quite a tale, ladies." The captain squinted her eyes at us. "What are you really hiding?"

"Nothing, I swear," Sunny said. "Look, at least give me a chance to prove myself. I can do a reading for you."

The captain looked doubtful. "Okay, I guess. What do I have to do?"

"May I hold your hat?" Sunny held out her hand.

The captain took off her hat and handed it to Sunny.

Sunny closed her eyes and concentrated, breathing deeply. After a few moments, she started talking. "Wow, you have a big family. Eight brothers, but none of them followed in their father's footsteps except you."

"That's public knowledge," Officer Justin chimed in, watching every move Sunny made. "Anyone could have found that out."

"True." Sunny concentrated harder on the captain. "You have a scar on your right thigh from a fishhook when you were little. You died your hair purple in high school. You're currently..." Sunny sucked in a breath. She motioned for the captain to lean in closer and then she whispered something in her ear.

The captain's eyes widened. "How did you know that? No one knows that."

Justin, Eddie, and Amy all looked at each other curiously.

"Because I really am psychic." Sunny handed the captain her hat back.

"And I read minds." I touched the captain's arm.

Her face paled. *If this gets out, it will ruin me.*

"It won't." I squeezed once, reassuring her.

She blinked but she didn't say a word.

"What won't?" Justin asked.

I ignored him and focused on the captain. "Think of a number between one and ten."

Eight. She sat with a blank face.

"Eight." I grinned.

She frowned. *That's a party trick.*

I raised a brow at her. "No trick."

I have on leopard print underwear. Bet you didn't know that. She crossed her legs and stared me down.

"I like leopard print as well, but I prefer solid colors." I leaned closer and whispered, "Especially for my underwear."

The captain sucked in a breath.

"I'm confused." Amy looked between the two of us. "What's happening?"

The captain yanked her arm back, giving both Sunny and me a wide berth. "Okay, I'm a believer."

"You are?" Amy gaped at her.

"I am indeed."

Amy shrugged. "Okay, then. If you're a believer, that's all I need to hear." Amy clapped her hands together and rubbed them as she looked Sunny and me over with renewed interest. "I think we could use their special talents with a few suspects I have my eyes on."

"Wait just a minute." Mitch stepped forward. "I don't think that's such a good idea."

"I didn't ask you." Amy narrowed her eyes.

"Look, this is a murder investigation we're talking about." Nik joined him. "I say we leave it to the professionals."

"I'm glad you agree, gentlemen." Captain Hughes stood and walked them out of her office and off the bridge. "We won't be needing your services. *These* professionals will do just fine. If Special Agent Randolph wants to enlist Kalli and Sunny as consultants, then I'm in full agreement. A killer is still on board, gentlemen. I'll do whatever I have to in order to solve this case. Let's get to work, ladies."

And with that, she closed the door, shutting them out, and we headed back into her office.

~

Sunny

The next morning, Mitch and I were sitting under an umbrella table with Nik and Kalli on the top deck. We'd all ordered coffee or tea, planning our day as we looked out over the ocean and contemplated our situation. Beautiful clear blue skies and calm waters.

You'd never know a murder investigation was going on.

Dallas the fitness director was setting up yoga mats by the pool. He spotted me and pulled out his imaginary fishing pole, casting it in my direction. I grabbed my heart as if I'd been caught and laughed. Dallas's face brightened, and he yanked his pole back and started to wind the reel.

Mitch turned steel gray eyes on him and stared.

Dallas cut his own line and quickly turned away.

"Alas, the one that got away was *this* big." I held my arms out as wide as my smile.

"There's plenty more fish in the sea." Mitch grunted.

"How long are you two going to pout?" I sipped my tea.

They'd both been cold and distant from us since we finally left the bridge and wouldn't tell them what we knew. We were sworn to silence regarding details about the case, and that was killing our handsome, troubled detectives.

"I'm not pouting." Mitch frowned. "Didn't sleep well. That's all." He took a big gulp of his steaming black coffee.

"Same." Nik rolled his head on his shoulders, chugged his own coffee, then winced and rubbed his lip.

"Kalli and I can't help that Captain Hughes asked us to consult with Special Agent Randolph?"

"That's right." Kalli nodded, wiping the rim of her cup three times and snapping her straw open before taking a sip of her own tea. "A captain is the highest form of law on a ship at sea. We had no choice but to follow her orders."

"If you hadn't given her a reading," Mitch said slowly to me, "or read her mind," he shot Kalli a meaningful look, "then none of this would have happened."

"Yeah, neither of you were supposed to work on this cruise," Nik pointed out, then held up his hands. "I'm just sayin'."

Kalli raised a brow. "You two should talk."

"Yes, but a murder happened. No matter what the captain says, we are *trained* for this very thing. We weren't at risk of getting hurt. You two, on the other hand, put yourselves in unnecessary danger more than once."

"Look, from what Kalli told me, you are a great detective," I said to Nik.

Nik's chest puffed out a smidge more than usual.

"And from what Sunny told me, you're pretty amazing at everything," Kalli said to Mitch.

One corner of Mitch's lips tipped up a hair before he cleared his throat.

"What we mean is no one doubts either of your competence, which is why neither of you like taking the back seat on a case. We get that. We know you guys don't like it, but we *do* have skills that none of you have." I raised my hands, palms up. "If there is even a slim chance that our abilities will help solve this case and get us all home to our families, then I'm all for it. How about you, Kalli?"

"I couldn't have said it better myself." She washed her hands with hand sanitizer.

"Okay, I'll play. Then what's the next step in the process?" Mitch eyed us both.

I bit my bottom lip. "We can't tell you."

"Is the bar open yet?" Nik looked around. "I think I need a shot of Baileys in my coffee."

"Here is something we *can* tell you." Kalli smiled wide with excitement. "Did you know that when a crime is committed on a cruise ship, the captain has to follow the law of the country it's closest to at the time of the crime? However, if the crime happens more than twelve miles offshore, then the captain has to follow the law of the country that made the ship. This particular ship was made in America, thank the Lord."

"Isn't that exciting?" I clapped my hands.

"Fascinating," Mitch said dryly.

"If the crime isn't serious, the captain can order the criminal to house arrest in the offender's cabin with posted guards," I went on. "But in this case, with a killer at large, the ship goes on lockdown."

"But don't you worry." Kalli pointed her finger at the men. "When the killer is caught, they will be incarcerated in a cell, a padded lockup room called a brig, with a steel toilet and sink, housed deep down in the non-passenger floors until the next port, thank the lord."

"*If* the killer is caught." Nik raised a brow.

"The captain's security officers can only do so much, and you've already met Eddie the ex-Belgian chief of police turned PI, and well, then there's Special Agent Randolph, who's quite lovely once you get past her tough exterior, I must say," I pointed out.

"The CVSSA aka Cruise Vessel Security & Safety Act requires the captain to report any serious crimes to the FBI, which is why Amy was summoned," Kalli added.

"There is no if," I said confidently. "It's definitely *when* now that they brought us on board."

"Well, good for you two." Nik raised his empty mug and saluted Mitch. "I predict our future won't be very bright, my friend."

My cell phone rang through the cruise app. "Sunny Stone here." My eyes widened. "Yes, she's right beside me." I nodded and looked at Kalli. "Right away, Captain." I hung up.

"What is it?" Kalli was already on her feet.

"There's been a break in the case." I surged to my feet to join her.

"About that shot," Mitch said to Nik. "I'm more than ready, but I might need something stronger than Baileys."

8

KALLI

We stood on the stage in Poseidon's Paradise, behind the closed curtain. My anxiety was at an all-time high as I listened to the theater fill with people. Meanwhile, Sunny was bebopping around like she didn't have a care in the world as she set up her fortune teller table. Captain Hughes had arranged for us to be an entertainment act, to get to the bottom of the break in the case.

Eddie was a watch aficionado himself and went with his gut on a hunch. He brought the watch to Crispin Aurelius at Nautical Elegance Jewelry & Gems boutique. He was a connoisseur of timepieces, whose expertise was sought by the elite across the world. He happened to love cruising and spent most of his time aboard various ships in their jewelry stores. He'd taken one look at Baron's watch and knew the truth immediately.

Baron Von Wielig's fancy timepiece was a fake.

"Are you ready?" Sunny asked me.

"No." I laughed, near hysteria. Our job was to target a few key suspects to see if they knew anything.

"You'll be fine." She patted my arm. "I'll sit at the

table, and you'll be my lovely assistant. When I'm giving someone a reading, I'll tell them we need to form a triangle for me to get an accurate reading since everyone's aura is off after traveling through The Bermuda Triangle."

"People will love that."

"I agree. You and I can sit beside each other, across from the subject, and each hold their hands, forming a triangle. Then I'll do the reading, and you can read their minds to get their honest reactions at the same time."

"As much as the thought of that makes me uncomfortable, this is actually a great idea," I said.

We took our places, and the curtains opened.

The dimly lit theater buzzed with excitement as the audience settled into their seats and their voices lowered to a hush of anticipation. Onstage, Sunny stood with an air of confidence and an aura of mystery. We'd raided the prop room, and she'd found enough items to form a traditional fortune-teller outfit that consisted of flowing layered clothing, scarves, shawls, jewelry, and a headpiece in various shades of purple.

I shuddered, imaging lice crawling through her short, pixie haircut.

The only other thing we found that would work for me as her assistant was a short pink sequined dress and feathers for my hair. At least the feathers weren't real and not nearly as bad as a headpiece, but I still cringed over the thought of who might have touched the comb currently shoved in my chignon.

As much as I wasn't a fan of the spa, I was desperate to de-germ myself the second this debacle was over with.

Beside Sunny, I tried to exude an air of calmness, filling my eyes with a glint of intrigue. Our fictional story was that we were a renowned duo, known for our psychic abilities that extended beyond the ordinary.

Mystical Mavens.

As the spotlight shone down, Sunny gazed into the crowd. "Ladies and gentlemen, welcome to an evening of revelations. Tonight, we delve into the depths of the mind to uncover truths hidden within."

I tried not to giggle. I knew firsthand she was the real deal, but I'd never seen her so dramatic. A born thespian. She was really hamming it up for the crowd, which actually made my nerves slightly dissipate.

I lowered my voice to a soothing hum as I chimed in, "Indeed, our minds hold the echoes of secrets, sometimes too faint for even ourselves to hear."

Sunny mouthed *nice* and then winked at me.

The crowd hushed, captivated by our words. The atmosphere crackled with energy, an unspoken yearning from the audience to be chosen for a reading, but we were looking for a sign. Among the spectators, a woman shifted uncomfortably, her nervous energy palpable.

Mystery Girl.

Sunny's gaze met mine, and I gave a slight nod. She was one of our main suspects when it came to Baron. With a graceful gesture, Sunny extended her hand toward Gracie. "Young lady, please join us on stage. Let us explore the whispers that dance across your thoughts."

Hesitant yet obviously intrigued, Gracie rose from her seat, her eyes flickering with curiosity and apprehension. She glanced around the audience a little nervously before climbing the steps to join Sunny and me under the spotlight.

"Let us sit, shall we?" Sunny gestured for Gracie to

sit at the table, and then Sunny and I took our seats across from her. "We need to join hands and form a triangle after passing through the Devil's playground and living to tell about it. This will restore your aura and keep us all protected and safe."

Gracie did as instructed and held out her hands until Sunny and I grasped them to form the triangle.

Instant electricity passed through us.

Has she thought anything yet? Sunny glanced at me.

I shook my head ever so slightly.

Sunny gazed into the woman's eyes, with a serene smile on her lips, trying to relax her. "Take a deep breath and allow your mind to open like a book. We are here only to reveal the truth and understand, not to judge."

You would if you knew what I did, Gracie thought.

I squeezed Sunny's hand, and she squeezed back.

Sunny closed her eyes and began to talk. "I see a troubled past. You have weathered many storms, especially after losing your mother during your birth. You've felt so alone."

Gracie sucked in a breath. "How did you know?"

"She's psychic," I whispered. "Just keep your mind open."

Gracie tried to relax. *Why did I agree to this? What if they find out?*

Sunny stayed focused and kept reading. "Your life hasn't been easy, but your future doesn't have to troubled if you unburden yourself. I see a path hidden beneath shadows; a connection severed by deceit. The weight of guilt lingers over a secret buried beneath layers of pretense."

Gracie's composure wavered, her eyes misting over. "I...I didn't mean for any of this to happen. It's all my fault," she confessed, her voice trembling. *I never should have told what I knew.* "I just wanted his attention. For once, I just wanted to know that he cared about me. That he loved me."

"We all want love. There's nothing wrong with that." Sunny opened her eyes, her gaze full of genuine compassion. "The truth you hold is a burden. Release it, for only then can healing begin."

I spoke in a soothing voice. "You are not defined by your mistakes, but by the choices you make moving forward. Tell us what you know. It will clear your conscience and make you feel better."

Gracie was already shaking her head no. "I can't. It's too dangerous." *He was right all along, but I didn't listen to him.* She let go of our hands. "I've said too much already." She surged to her feet as if just now remembering an entire audience was watching her. She gasped and then ran off the stage.

Sunny looked at me in shock as the audience stared at us with bated breath, waiting for our next move. I didn't need to touch her to know she was thinking, *What do we do now?*

"And there you have it. She is cured!" I smiled wide and took a deep bow.

For the next thirty minutes, we discovered way more than we wished to know about our fellow passengers, but nothing useful for the murder investigation. Finally, our shift was over. We stepped back and signaled for the curtain to close as disappointed mutters mixed with applause sounded behind the curtain.

"Cured?" Sunny gaped at me. "We're not apothecaries."

I shrugged. "What can I say, I get nervous under pressure."

"Well, we didn't find out anything about Baron's

watch being a fake, but we did find something very interesting about Gracie."

"That she was in love with him. I heard her thoughts." I scrubbed my hands with hand sanitizer. "I thought she was in love with Lance or even Frankie, but apparently not. I heard her say she regretted telling what she knew to someone, and she should have listened to him because he had been right all along. I'm not sure who that *him* is either. Who is she in danger from that she can't say anything more? I think she thought we were fakes but after you knew about her mother, she was genuinely worried about us finding out the truth. Whatever that is."

"We have so many questions still, but you're right about one thing." Sunny nodded. "She was in love with Baron, but not like you think."

I puckered my brow. "What do you mean?"

"You might have heard her thoughts, but I *saw* her past. I saw the truth." Sunny looked me in the eye. "Gracie Marks is Baron Von Wielig's daughter."

Sunny

"Oh shoot." Kalli reached her hand up and touched the top of her head. "The clip to my feathers must have fallen off my head on the stage. The feathers got caught in my sequins, but I need the clip to fix it. Ugh, that means I have to go back out there. Cross your fingers I don't get rotten tomatoes thrown at me. I'll meet you in the dressing room shortly," she said, walking toward the curtains on the stage.

I thought about what Gracie had said and what I had seen. She wanted her father's love but never felt like she got it. If she hadn't run off, I would have told her the last thoughts before he died were of how much he loved her. That he needed to fix things because it wasn't fair to her. Fix what? Did he have enemies? Is that why she was worried about getting into trouble if she told what she knew?

Who was she in danger from?

The audience was growing restless, waiting for the next act. What on earth was taking Kalli so long? I was about to head out there and stall while I helped her look.

Oh, no.

The curtains suddenly opened, and Kalli was on her hands and knees, searching the stage for the comb that went to her feather headpiece. She scrambled to her feet when Lance the magician, clad in a shimmering black suit, confidently walked onto the stage. She looked at me with raised eyebrows.

I watched from the side of the stage, helpless to do anything else.

We'd never officially met Lance. Even if he'd seen Kalli around the ship, she looked totally different in the sparkly mini dress, her hair up in a fancy twist, and a face full of more makeup than I'd ever seen her wear.

Spotting Kalli, he grinned and approached her, slipping his arm around her and bowing to the audience. "And here she is, folks. My new assistant! Isn't she a looker?" he exclaimed; his voice laced with excitement. He looked down at her as if deep in thought before finally adding, "Ready to make some magic happen?"

Her eyes widened and she stepped back and hissed, "Excuse me, sir. That is totally inappropriate.

And no, I am not ready to do that or anything else with you," but apparently not quietly enough.

The audience laughed.

Lance's smile stiffened as he whispered, "I'm not into improv. I asked for a professional. Just follow my lead."

I could hear him since I was right by the curtains, stage left.

Kalli's eyebrows furrowed in confusion. "Look, I don't want to ruin your act, so I'll play along for now, but I really don't know what you're talking about," she whispered back through her stiff smile and struck a pose like a flamingo with raised wings as she stood beside him and faced the audience. "I'm not an assistant."

"Then why are you wearing the costume meant for *my* assistant and standing on the stage during *my* show?" He walked around her, then pushed an ornate box at the center of the stage in a big circle, showing it to the audience in dramatic fashion.

She just stood there for a moment then flapped her arms like a pelican taking flight, adding the running man with her feet as if she felt like she should be moving as well. "I needed a costume for my psychic show right before yours. This was all I could find."

"Then you owe me one." He caught her arm mid flap and took her hand in his own, making her cringe. She pasted on a smile and didn't let go, no matter how much I knew it killed her. Walking her around the box, he stopped right in front of it then lifted the lid. "Isn't she a gem, folks?"

The audience clapped wildly, with a few whistles to boot.

Her face flushed pink.

"Let's show them what a team player you are." He

stared her in the eyes. "Just hop in the box, sweetheart, and we'll make some real magic right here in front of our fabulous audience." He looked at her once over.

She clenched her jaw. "Keep thinking those thoughts, *darling*, and I'll make you disappear for good. You're not the only one with tricks up their sleeve." Kalli winked at the audience as she let go of his hand and stepped inside the box.

The audience roared with laughter even louder.

As the magician began to close the box, Kalli's face registered her anxiety. She mouthed, *Help me*, probably hoping I would intervene.

I nodded, trying to think of what I could do without being obvious and blowing our cover.

"Wait, please listen!" she implored, her voice tinged with desperation. "I changed my mind. What did you use to clean this? Oh, God, it smells like body odor." She gagged.

She would need therapy after this.

Lance was clearly caught up in his own performance because he ignored her pleas. He brandished a saw, poised to glide it through the box and divide her in half.

Kalli let out a scream, looking horrified, then her fear gave way to a torrent of words. "You can't saw a human body in half! It's impossible! The mess would be horrendous. The organs, the blood vessels—"

Lance came out of his stupor and hesitated as her words registered. A quizzical expression crossed his face. "What are you talking about?"

The audience was glued to the two of them, hanging on every word.

Kalli continued; her voice now tinged with panic. "And those knives! How many germs are on them? Have you even washed them? There could be a million bacteria! I could get a serious infection and die. Do you really want that on your conscience? I'll haunt you, I promise I will, if my ma and Aunt Tasoula don't put a curse on you first."

"This is all fake. Don't you know anything? If I sawed through your body for real, wouldn't you be dead anyway?" His frustration was clearly evident after he realized what he'd said out loud. "But since I *am* going to saw through you for real, because this is real, and I am a master of magic," he said louder for the audience's sake, "any last words?"

"Yes! You're insane, and I heard your thoughts. I have dirt on you, you dirty man, so I suggest you let... me...out...now!" Her voice rose so high I swear I heard glass break somewhere.

He hesitated a moment over her words, making me wonder if there really was dirt to be had on him.

Figuring this was my chance to intervene, I strolled out on the stage with my arms flowing at my sides. I still had my fortune teller costume on, and I had grabbed my lit sage. "Abradabradoo, shazam, ala-cazoo...unhand this woman, or I'll put a curse on you!" I twirled about, spreading the smoke in eerie circles.

Lance's eyes widened as he dropped the saw and stepped back with his hands raised. "You two are in-sane. She's all yours." He turned and left the stage, post haste.

"Thank you," Kalli whispered.

"Of course. We're partners, remember?" I whispered back, making a big deal of unlocking the box and helping Kalli step out. *Does he really have dirt,* I thought.

"Mud," she whispered and took a bow.

I joined her, saying loudly, "And just like that, she is cured." We backed off the stage once more.

This time the applause was thunderous.

"Guess our second act was an even bigger hit," I said.

"There had better not be a third," said two male voices we both knew well from behind us. I didn't have to be psychic to *detect* their anger.

At that moment, I really wished I could make us disappear.

9

KALLI

Natalia rinsed the cleansing treatment from my hair as I lay back in the salon chair with my head over the sink. Back home, Aunt Tasoula had a special cape she kept just for me, and she always sanitized the salon chair before my appointment at her shop, Hara's Halo. I never color my hair or put products on my body because of all the chemicals. But after being Lance's *assistant*, I felt the need for a full-body scrub from head to toe to de-germ myself.

Nik and Mitch were not happy with Sunny and me. They wanted answers now that our safety was in question. We'd promised we would fill them in but had bought ourselves some time, saying we had already booked salon services. Lucky for us, Natalia and Ivan had squeezed us in.

Natalia had been very understanding about my odd sanitary requests.

"Wow, you're really thorough on washing my hair." Her hands felt like they were scrubbing my scalp off.

"Almost done, just a little longer." *Oh, no, no, no. How is this happening? What do I do? This wasn't meant for her. She is going to be so mad at me.*

I grabbed her hands to still them. "What did you do?"

She gasped and yanked her hands away. "How did you know?"

"Sit me up. I need to see..." My voice trailed off as I came to an upright position and gaped at myself in the mirror.

"I'm so sorry." Natalia wrung her hands together, shaking her head over and over. "This wasn't supposed to happen."

My hair was still wet, so the color was darker than what it would be once it dried, but there was no mistaking the shade.

"Green?" I sputtered. "I have green hair? I've never colored my hair in my life. All I wanted was to kill any germs lingering on my hair and body." I couldn't stop thinking about the thousands of chemicals in hair dyes, including endocrine-disrupting compounds, carcinogens, and aromatic amines soaking into my brain.

My scalp tingled. What did that mean?

Oh, Zeus. What if I was bleeding out through my scalp?

Sunny popped her head out from under the dryer. Natalia and Ivan were both trained in all areas of the spa. "Green hair? What?" Her eyes sprang wide. "Oh, my." She covered her mouth with her hand. "At least it makes your eyes pop."

"You need to stay under the dryer a little longer," Ivan said.

"In a minute." She hopped out of her chair and skirted around him, her pretty pink flamingo cape flapping like wings with her every movement.

"I look like a troll!" I wailed, twisting my under-

water garden of seaweed cape. Figures, I'd get the seaweed cape. I had the worst luck.

"Nik certainly can't say you didn't try something
new." Sunny bit her bottom lip. "It might be pretty
when it dries."

"I'm getting paid back by karma," Natalia
whispered.

"What do you mean?" I narrowed my eyes.

"Nothing," Natalia said, her face flushing a deep
rose.

"You spoke out loud." Sunny crossed her arms and
stared at Natalia. "We kind of know you meant *something*, so you might as well spill it."

Natalia sat down and started crying. "I really am
sorry, Miss Kalli."

Ivan patted her back, looking helpless.

"It's fine," I lied, but I didn't want to make her feel
worse than she obviously already did. "What happened?" I asked softly.

"Lance." She threw her hands up, and Ivan
dropped his. She stood and started to pace. "You already know he cheated on me with his assistant, Chee
Chee. She quit when she realized he was just using
her, so I thought he could come back to me."

"Excuse me," Ivan interjected with his head
hanging a bit lower. "I have to restock the stations for
our next guests. Angela is getting a quick tune-up before her next theater show." He quickly disappeared.

"Lance is not worthy of you." Sunny watched as
Ivan disappeared from view. "Sometimes the one
you're meant to be with is right in front of you."

I handed Natalia a box of tissues.

"I can't even think about another man right now."
She blew her nose. "I feel so stupid. I need to heal my
heart. Lance has already moved on."

"With Cara the auctioneer?" I asked.

"I don't think so." Natalia lifted one shoulder. "I thought so at first, but now I think he was just using us all. Lately, I've seen him hanging out with Gracie a lot more than Cara. I knew he was a ladies' man, but I didn't think he was a cradle robber. I just don't understand what he thinks I'm missing."

"You're not missing anything. You're beautiful, both inside and out. There's nothing wrong with you. I think you're right. He's just using people to get what he wants." Sunny narrowed her eyes. The question is what exactly does he want?"

"Where does the green dye come in?" I touched my hair that had begun to dry and looked even more hideous.

Like a neon troll.

Natalia looked at me sheepishly. "I used to trim and style Lance's hair. He's not a natural blond." She rolled her eyes. "I admit it. I wanted revenge, so I put the green dye in the bottle I use for his touch ups, not realizing the bottle looks a lot like the one with the treatment solution I just used on you. I grabbed the wrong bottle by mistake." She raised her hands, palms up. "Karma got me. The dye is temporary, I promise. It will wash out in a couple days." She grabbed my hand. "Obviously, there's no charge for today. Please let me make this up to you with another service." *I'm so getting fired over this.*

"No one's getting fired." I patted her hand.

She let go, and her eyes widened as she gaped at me warily.

"I mean, I'm okay. No one needs to know this wasn't my decision. Like you said, it's only temporary. I did promise to try new things. Who knows, I might even grow to like the look." Who was I kidding? That would *never* happen in this lifetime or any other. "I really don't need any other services but thank you." I shuddered at the thought of anything else touching my body except my own products.

"Okay, thank you." Natalia looked around. "I don't know where Ivan went. I'll finish up with Sunny, and then you ladies are all set. Thank you so much for being so kind to me, and for listening to my troubles."

"You're very welcome," Sunny said.

"Don't you worry," I added. "We're all too happy to figure out what Magic Man Lance is up to."

Sunny

"You ready to talk now?" Mitch asked as I approached the table that he and Nik had saved for us in The Wheelhouse bar.

He handed me a Tequila Sunrise. Kalli had suggested we meet the men there, claiming she was in dire need of a chardonnay. I had requested something sunny. I took the drink and sat down.

"All I can say is it has been a day." I took a sip of my fruity drink and sighed.

"I take it there was an issue with your de-germing, judging by the tone in my girlfriend's voice when she requested I have her drink of choice ready for her by the time you ladies joined us." He looked around. "Where is she, anyway?"

"The ladies' room." Sunny gestured toward the door.

Nik looked in that direction, then blew out a long whistle and signaled our waitress.

Courtney walked over, wearing a puzzled expression on her face. "Is something wrong with your drinks?"

"I think we're going to need the nine-ounce pour after all." Nik handed the six-ounce glass to the waitress.

Courtney followed the direction of his gaze. "Ah, gotcha," she said, spotting Kalli. "For the record, I love the neon green," she said as Kalli reached our table. "I almost chose that exact shade but went with aqua blue tips instead." She shrugged. "I think you look like a rockstar. I'll be right back with your wine."

"Thank you." Kalli sat down with a straight back and perfect posture, keeping her smile planted firmly in place as Brie and Haden snapped her picture.

"Now, this is a story I have got to hear," Nik said as soon as they left, a devilish grin spreading wide across his godly face.

She smoothed the fabric of her dark purple sundress, which was a bold and vibrant contrast to the neon green shade of her hair. Her dark green eyes popped as she pulled her collapsible Barbie straw out of her bra pocket, then took a dainty sip of her water before replying. "I don't have a clue what you're talking about. There's no story. I'm just trying new things like you suggested."

I stared at her in awe. She had completely transformed from the hot mess she'd been just thirty minutes ago. Only Kalli could make neon green hair look stunning and classy.

"Yeah, I'm not buying that for a second, Ballas." Nik reached out and brought her hand to his lips then kissed it. His eyes shimmered with thoughts for her mind only.

She blushed, pulling her hand out of his grasp and

clearing her throat. "I'm glad you like it, Detective, but don't get too used to it. It's temporary."

Courtney brought her a bigger glass of chardonnay. "Here you go, sweetie. Enjoy." She winked and walked away over to the bar where Rafe had signaled her. He waved to us then turned to Angela the theater star, who looked fabulous after her touch up. Brie and Haden snapped a picture of them, and then they dove back into animated conversation. Good for him. He'd certainly gotten a lot more confident than when we'd first met him on the island.

Kalli transferred her straw and held up her glass in a salute then took a big sip.

"Tink here has worn a few interesting looks herself." Mitch winked at me before taking a sip of his beer.

"Very funny, Detective." I ran my fingertips over my short pixie style haircut, remembering, and couldn't disagree with my husband.

Back in Divinity my hair stylist, Raoulle, loved to talk with his hands while he cut hair. The more worked up he got, the crazier the hair style turned out. I'd learned to invoke my fifth amendment right and remain silent if I wanted to walk out of the salon with anything longer than a buzz cut.

"In all seriousness, what happened today?" Nik sipped whiskey in a rocks glass.

"I can't even go there." Kalli shuddered, looking ill.

I sighed. "Okay, look. If I've learned anything over the years, it's that Mitch and I work better together than apart, so I'm going to tell you what we know. No matter what the captain said, I know there's no way either of you have been sitting around doing nothing, so I expect you to give us the same courtesy."

Mitch winked, and Nik nodded.

"Okay, then. When we got the call about a break in the case, we found out that Baron's expensive timepiece was a fake," I said.

"Interesting," Mitch said. "How can you be so sure."

I pulled my own little handy dandy notebook out of my fringed satchel, and Mitch's eyes crinkled at the corners with obvious amusement. I ignored that as I continued and looked in my book. "There's an expert on the ship who verified it. Crispin Aurelius."

"Elton the entertainer knows a thing or two about watches. He collects them himself. That evening after his show, he was admiring the real one Baron was wearing. They were sitting right beside me. Why would Baron have a fake watch when he can clearly afford a real one?" Nik rubbed his whiskered jaw.

"When I got a reading off Baron's corpse, he said he wanted to fix things." I shrugged. "He said it wasn't fair to her. She was all he had left, and she would never know how much he loved her."

"Who?" Mitch asked. "He was with so many women, I would never guess he was in love."

"Because he wasn't in love with a woman romantically," Kalli said. "He was in love with his only child. A daughter by the name of Gracie Marks, aka Mystery Girl."

"Wow, so that was why we saw her coming out of his cabin." Mitch wrote a few notes down in his own little notebook.

"There were obviously issues between them. We saw them arguing at the pool and in the shops on the island," I added.

"Captain Hughes arranged for us to have an act at the theater. We called ourselves Mystical Mavens," Kalli said.

"We saw," Mitch said dryly, raising a brow at me.

"Hey, I was only working because the captain asked me to."

"How convenient. And how is it the captain is suddenly a true believer when she started out a skeptic?"

"Because I saw she's having an affair with a crew member, which is frowned upon on this cruise line. She's worried about both of them getting fired."

"Really? Who is it?" Nik asked.

"I promised her I wouldn't tell a soul, and I intend to keep that promise." I nodded once. It wasn't my place to reveal her love life to anyone.

"When my wife makes a promise, she doesn't break it. It's one of the things I love most about her."

"That's admirable. Where we come from, secrets are nearly impossible to keep." Nik chuckled.

"Our Greek families do love to gossip." Kalli laughed and shook her head. "Anyway, I heard Gracie's thoughts. She was worried about us finding out the truth. Then she said she never should have told someone what she knew. And finally, that she should have listened to him. He was right all along."

"That's a lot to unpack, Ballas." Nik frowned.

"Exactly. She could have been talking about more than one person, and we don't know who *he* was that she referred to. She ran off before we could question her."

"So, how did you end up in Lance's magic act?" Nik asked.

"He mistook me for his new assistant because I was wearing her outfit. I had no clue when we raided the wardrobe closet, and that was all I could find."

"I have to say I liked *that* look a lot." Nik waggled his eyebrows.

"Trust me, so did Lance. You don't want to know what *his* thoughts were." She shuddered.

Nik frowned.

"You said you had dirt on him. What was it?" I asked.

"I bluffed. The only dirt I had on him were his dirty thoughts." Kalli cringed. "That's all the news we have for now."

"It's your turn, Detectives." I looked at Mitch and Nik. "I know you've got something, so spill it."

"Mavis is out of the medical center," Nik said. "Turns out she had a mild heart attack. They have her stabilized and on medication, but she'll need to see her cardiologist when we finally get off this ship."

"Meanwhile, Milton is back in the casino as usual. The man wins as much as he loses but then puts his money right back into the games. I think he might have a problem." Mitch looked at me. "Since we're still on lockdown and within range of cell towers, I managed to get a call through to my buddy back home. He's looking into Milton's background for me. He says he's from money and they travel all the time, but something doesn't add up. He's changed his story a few times about his background whenever I bring it up. Either he's going senile, or he's lying."

"Well, I'm glad Mavis is doing better. She had us worried," Kalli said.

"Same here." I breathed a sigh of relief. "Anything else?"

They looked at each other and seemed to come to a silent agreement.

Mitch finally said, "The prized piece of art that was meant to be the finale to the art auction is missing."

10

KALLI

Sunny and I walked into the captain's office during a heated dispute.

"If I could get off this ship right now, I would quit." Cara tucked her wavy shoulder length auburn hair behind her shoulder as she looked up at the tall captain from her short height. "I don't need this kind of aggravation. I was just doing my job." She placed her hands on her curvy hips.

"You're the art auctioneer," Diana North said. "You're not the event planner. That falls under my duties as the cruise director." She looked at Captain Hughes and crossed her arms over her chest, waiting.

The captain rubbed her temples then looked at Officer Justin, Agent Amy, PI Eddie, and First Officer Tyrone. They all shrugged, deferring to her as the highest-ranking officer on the ship. She sighed and looked back at the women. "Ladies, we're in the middle of a murder investigation. Can't you find a way to work together on this?"

Diana was nearly the captain's height. She arched a sleek black brow and shook her head slightly. "Seriously?" She inhaled deeply then blew out a long, slow breath before replying, "I am just trying to do my job as well. There is no *working together* with this woman. She's impossible."

"Because you want to cancel everything. You're so stubborn, you refuse to listen, and you won't let anyone help. Poor Simon doesn't know what to do with himself now that the excursions are all cancelled during lockdown. Would it kill you to give him a job?" Cara threw her hands up. "And I'm more than capable of just being an auctioneer. You might know about events, but I know about art auctions. Just because Mr. Von Wielig is dead, it doesn't mean the art auction can't still go on. His client deserves that much."

"I agree," Diana ground out. "However, we can't exactly have an auction if the big reveal isn't anywhere to be found. It's a good thing I checked your inventory. You missed that very important item."

"I didn't miss anything." Cara looked as if she wanted to stomp her foot. "I've worked with Baron before. He always hides the prized piece himself and doesn't tell anyone where it is for security reasons. No one expected for him to be murdered. That's why that piece is accounted for on my inventory list because Baron knew where it was. I can't help it no one else did. And now the auction is at risk because you won't let the show go on."

"This is ridiculous," Diana said. "A *correct* inventory is also needed for security reasons."

"Which is exactly why you went to see Captain Hughes." Cara scowled. "You're just jealous that Baron liked me more than you, and now you're trying to get me in trouble. Two can play this game. I just might have a few words to say to her about you as well."

Diana barked out a laugh. "Don't flatter yourself. I had to see the captain about another matter that had nothing to do with you, but I'm finished. She's all yours." Diana swept her hand toward the captain, then walked past Cara with her head held high as she marched herself all the way off the bridge.

Captain Hughes walked over to her office door and held it open. "I'm sorry, Ms. Carmichael, but my next meeting is here." She glanced at Sunny and me then back to Cara. "You'll have to make an appointment if there's anything else."

"I don't need to tattle on anyone, Captain." Cara stood a little straighter, but that didn't help much. "I'm perfectly capable of handling my problems all on my own like an adult." With that, she turned and stormed off the bridge.

"This is turning out to be one never-ending nightmare of a cruise. Remind me never to sail into the Bermuda Triangle again." The captain held the door. "Tyrone, can you man the bridge?"

He nodded once. "Aye Aye, Captain." Then he left and the captain shut the door.

"You wanted to see us?" Sunny asked.

"Yes. Have a seat, ladies. Please." She eyed my hair with a raised silver eyebrow.

I prayed she wouldn't ask about it. My prayers were answered as the captain sat at the head of a boardroom meeting style table. Justin and Eddie sat on one side, and Amy sat on the other end. Meanwhile, Sunny and I sat on the other side.

"How can we help?" I asked.

"For one, you can stop telling your husband and boyfriend about the case," Amy said, wearing her special agent hat for sure.

I sucked in a little breath and held it. How did they know we told the guys about Baron's watch being a fake?

"No one was supposed to know a piece of the art from the auction was missing," Justin Cho said.

Phew. I released the breath I held.

"I know you only asked for our help because we have a unique set of skills we bring to the table, but you forget something," Sunny said. "Our men are detectives and very good at their jobs. They've each solved several murder cases. You verified Baron's watch was a fake, but we didn't know anything about the missing art."

"Yeah, they came to us about that," I added. "I know you don't want to involve too many people, but we're working with a ticking clock here. If you ask me, I think we could use all the help we can get."

"I don't think—" Amy started to say.

"I couldn't agree more," Eddie said.

Amy frowned at him.

Captain Hughes nodded. "I agree. This case is becoming bigger than all of us."

"But—" Amy started.

"Look, Amy, I know you don't like it, but I trust Eddie. And Kalli and Sunny have been right about everything so far. I don't always approve of their *unique* methods, but they have been getting results and providing useful clues. If their men can add helpful perspectives and bring their resources and connections to the table as well, then we'll all be better off. The safety of this crew and every passenger is my top priority."

Eddie looked us each in the eye and added, "None of us are safe with a killer still on the loose."

∽

Sunny

Kalli and I joined Nik and Mitch up on the Sky Deck. We sat at the bar like we had the first night we met, in the same seats where I had discovered she could read minds and had told her I was psychic. The same knot that had filled me with dread had blossomed into full-fledged doom and gloom.

Murder tended to do that to me.

Eddie was right. We needed all the help we could get. The thought of a killer still walking free around the ship terrified me, even more so now that I was a mother. I had to stop being reckless and think about my children.

Granny Gert was too old to raise them, and there was no way I wanted my own mother to bring them up. Babysit whenever we needed them, yes. Raise them permanently? No way. My parents were too old as well.

I should have made a will before this trip.

I would have designated my best friend Jo and her husband Cole. They had twin boys, and they were amazing parents. Or Jo's cousin Zoe and her husband Sean were expecting a daughter. I just knew they were going to be great parents as well. I wrung my hands, letting my doubts fill me with anxiety.

Why had I insisted on this trip?

If anything happened to us, how our children turned out in the future would be all my fault. Mitch would be mad at me for eternity, and I would be forced to haunt everyone. I should have just stayed home instead of rocking the boat, literally.

"You okay?" Kalli asked, her hair still green but a little more blond and a little less neon now. "I recognize the beginning of a panic attack more than anyone."

I took a deep breath. "I'm okay. This case is just getting to me."

"I agree. Eddie reminding us that we still have a killer on the loose hit home."

"Ladies, how have you been liking the cruise so far?" Frankie asked with a wide smile and a twinkle in his eyes. "Looks like it's been eventful." He eyed Kalli's hair.

"It certainly has been." Kalli ran a hand over the strands.

"I heard you were a hit at your show. I had no idea you two were so *gifted*." He winked, and it was obvious he thought we were fakes.

"We're always up for a little fun," I said.

"And the tips don't hurt, I imagine." He chuckled.

"People love a good party trick." Kalli laughed, playing along.

She'd told me the reason she didn't tell people in her hometown of Clearview Connecticut that she could read minds was because it wasn't her profession, and she hadn't been born with the ability. It was caused by a freak accident. She didn't think anyone would believe her, and her family would worry about her even more than they already did. She didn't want anyone to freak out and not trust her anymore, thinking she was always reading their minds. So, she found it more useful if people didn't know about her ability.

That way they let their guard down.

"Except for Gracie Marks," I added.

Everyone in Divinity knew that I was a psychic because being a fortune teller was my profession. Not everyone was a true believer, but at least I didn't have to hide anything. I could still read them whether they believed in me or not.

"She was a little shaken up after her reading," I continued. "You know, with so many of her secrets being revealed."

Frankie's smile slipped a little. "She told you her secrets?"

"She didn't need to," Kalli replied. "Mystical Mavens, remember?"

"Right." He laughed, but it didn't sound as hearty. If anything, he seemed a little unnerved. "What can I get you, ladies? My shift's about to end."

"I'll have a widow maker." I watched him closely.

He cleared his throat. "Interesting choice."

"You know what? I'll have the same," Kalli said, adding, "I'm all about trying new things these days."

"I can see that. Coming right up." He headed down the counter to get the grenadine syrup, vodka, Jägermeister herbal liqueur, and Kahlua coffee liqueur.

Courtney stopped by our stools. "Don't mind him. He's just worried Gracie's secret might involve him because he's married with children, yet he isn't above doing almost anything in the name of a good tip. He makes me sick. One of these days, karma is going to catch up to him, if it hasn't already." She glared daggers at him before pasting on another beaming smile and heading off to wait on more customers.

I'd known he irritated her, but I had no idea how much she genuinely disliked him. "This day just keeps getting more and more interesting," I said.

"There you are, ladies." A new bartender delivered our drinks and then moved on down the bar.

"That's different. What did you order?" Mitch hopped off his stool and walked over to see what I had with Nik hot on his heels.

"A widow maker." I smiled and took a yummy sip.

Mitch blinked.

"Same." Kalli giggled and wiped her glass three times.

Nik frowned.

"Are you two trying to tell us something?" Mitch drew his brows together.

"Yes, and you're going to be so happy." I beamed, prolonging the anticipation, yet dying to tell them.

"Captain Hughes wants you both to join our team and work on the case with us," Kalli dropped the bomb.

The men stood up a little straighter.

"It's about time they came to their senses and hired some real professionals," Nik said. "Detectives with actual degrees in the criminal justice system and real-life experience in solving murder cases."

"Don't make me regret telling you, Nikos." Kalli narrowed her eyes.

"Never." He kissed her cheek. "I'm just thrilled I get to work beside my incredibly gifted girlfriend."

"Nice save." Kalli stared him down. "Just know I'm watching you."

"Why, that's the best thing I've heard all day." Nik blinked his baby blues, wearing the most innocent expression.

Kalli rolled her eyes but couldn't stop the corners of her lips from tipping up.

"And don't *you* make me regret going to bat for you both." I poked Detective Grumpy Pants in the chest.

"I always appreciate everything you do." He caught my hand and kissed it. "I just have one question."

"What's that?" I smiled, looking up at him.

My smile faded away and I sucked in a breath as a wave of despair swept over me so suddenly, it took my breath away. It felt like a black cloud seeping through my pores and suffocating my every cell with pure evil.

Something bad was about to happen.

"Sunny, did you hear me?" Mitch asked. "Are you okay?"

"I'll be fine." I looked around but didn't see anything amiss. "Just a wave of negative energy coming from somewhere on this ship."

Mitch frowned. "How soon can we start?"

"Not soon enough."

11

KALLI

"What's so urgent?" I asked Sunny as I opened the door to my room.

"You forgot your purse up on the Sky Deck." She handed it to me.

"I can't believe I did that. It's so unlike me." I took the bag from her and set it aside to be sanitized, thoroughly. "Oh, lord, maybe the chemicals from the green dye really have started to affect my brain. There's no other explanation."

"Or maybe you're just tired," Sunny pointed out gently. "This has been one roller coaster of a week."

"Maybe." I took a deep breath to calm myself down. "Thank you so much. Was there something else?"

"Yes. I know it's not the most ideal time, but this can't wait until morning. Can I come in?"

And just like that my heart rate spiked once more.

"Who's here, Ballas?" Nik was in the bedroom of our balcony suite, watching TV before bed.

"Sunny brought my purse. I'll just be a minute," I hollered back to him.

"Take your time." I heard him already chuckling. "They have all my favorite sitcoms on the menu."

"We're good." I stepped back and gestured for her to enter.

"Do you have any wine? We can sit on the balcony." She winced. "Trust me. You're going to want some when you hear what I have to tell you."

"Oh boy." My stomach flipped. What could possibly happen next? "You can head on out. I'll be right behind you."

Sunny headed out on the balcony, and I poured us each a glass of wine. With our drink package, we had a full bar in our suite. Bedroom, living room, jacuzzi bathroom, and balcony. Nik had spared no expense in getting us the best room to convince me to go on this cruise with him.

I should have trusted my gut and stayed home.

I carried our drinks out to the balcony. The clouds twinkled in the dark sky and ocean waves gently lapped at the side of the boat down below. It was soothing, even though I was still worried about ending up in Davy Jones's locker. Sitting in a fancy wrought iron chair, I handed a glass to Sunny who sat in the seat on the other side of the bistro table.

"What, no Barbie straw?" She eyed me curiously.

"No need," I took a sip straight from the glass, "I trust my own dish washing. Restaurants, not so much."

"Gotcha." She sipped her drink as well. "I have to say, I'm becoming a fan of that pink straw. It's like one of those collapsible metal canes, but Barbie-sized. It's so convenient."

"And sanitary, not to mention good for the environment." I studied Sunny impatiently with curiously. "I love your company, and all, but what was so important you had to come to my room this late?"

"Okay, here goes. So, when I picked up your purse, I got a reading off of it."

"You did?"

Her eyes met mine and held. "Yes, and you're not going to like it."

"Past, present, or future?" I held up my hand. "Because learning about who I might have been in a past life would be cool. Or having you tell me something I already know from my past would be validating. But having you predict what is about to happen in the future is just plain terrifying."

"Well, I'm not really sure." She studied me curiously. "Did your purse belong to your mom by any chance?"

"Yes, ma had it for years. Pop just bought her a new one she likes better, so she gave me this one because she knows how much I love vintage Gucci." I stopped short and stared at Sunny, suddenly understanding the reading wasn't about me. It was about Ma. "What's wrong with Ma?" My mind began jumping to any and all conclusions.

"It's not scary or anything." Sunny's voice held a note of calm before she paused and tilted her head as she thought out loud, "Or, well, maybe it *is* scary. I guess how you look at the situations could be."

"Situations? Okay, I can't take it. Just tell me." I tipped my glass, taking a larger sip, eager for her to spill the tea on the fate of my poor Ma.

"It's like that movie Planes, Trains, and Automobiles."

My lips parted, and I stared at her, confused. "Wait, my reading is about businessmen who have travel problems?"

"No, but it is about a mismatched crazy pair of characters who get into a bunch of misadventures while trying to get somewhere. Only they're not trying to get home." Sunny stared at me. "They're trying to get to you."

I slapped my forehead. "Oh, Zeus, what have Ma and Aunt Tasoula done now?" So that was what they'd been trying to tell me between all that static! I glanced at my nearly empty wine glass and thought I may need the entire bottle before this tale was over.

"Well, first they rented a boat." Sunny scoffed. "That didn't go over so well with your pop when they crashed it before even leaving the harbor."

"You're kidding?" I gaped at her. "How did they talk their way out of that one?"

"Um, no, not kidding." She shook her head. "And they told him they were going fishing for that night's special. My family lives in Divinity. That's about five hours from New York City. Clearview, however, is only about one hour away."

I was already shaking my head. "But they don't fish. Or have a boating license. They must have taken Pop's."

"Exactly."

I rubbed my aching temples, no longer worried about dying from the chemicals in the hair dye. Ma and Aunt Tasoula were going to kill me first. I sighed. "You said *first*, so I take it there's more?"

She nodded with another wince. "Told you that you would want the drink."

We both sipped long and deep.

"Next, they signed up for scuba diving lessons. I couldn't make this up if I tried. They nearly drowned when they passed the guide and tried to head out of the harbor to swim to the cruise ship on one tank."

"What in all of Mount Olympus were they thinking?" My family had taken their craziness to a whole new level.

"They told your pop that you inspired them to take a vacation. He wasn't buying it any more than we are. Needless to say, they are banned from scuba diving for life."

I groaned. "Please tell me that was all."

"Nope. Guess they decided both *on* the water and *in* the water wasn't working. So, they went deep *under* the water. They signed up for an adventure submarine tour of the coral reef. They tried to take over the sub and head out to sea."

All I could do was shake my head in disbelief. "They must have been arrested for that one for sure."

"Nope. Your ma claimed dementia, and your aunt flirted with the submarine captain. It worked because he didn't press charges, and your aunt scored a date." Sunny held her hands up. "Apparently, she's on a break with her boyfriend."

"I told you my family is crazy."

"Oh, I'm not done yet." She shook her head.

I stared in sheer amazement at my newfound friend, every scene of the Dynamic Duo playing through my head, probably damaging my brain cells. I finally found my voice. "What more could there possibly be?"

She paused a beat. "They took to the air next."

"Wait, what?" I gaped at her. "Please tell me they didn't highjack an airplane."

"No, but they *did* highjack a parasailing crew."

I closed my eyes. "Oh, no."

"Oh, yes." It was clear she was trying not to laugh. "They rigged your aunt up while your ma rode shotgun on the boat. She tipped them big to take them out further into the ocean. When they did, your ma cut the rope. She honestly thought the parachute would keep your aunt in the air until she reached the cruise ship."

I couldn't believe the lengths my family would go to in order to *save* me. "That's impossible without a boat pulling it."

"Exactly. Your aunt was lucky the Coast Guard was roaming the area she landed in." Sunny pointed at the ocean. "And even more lucky there weren't any sharks around. They're being spotted more often now, even during non-feeding times."

"I know. Global warming is a real thing." I dreaded hearing the answer to my next question. "Surely, they must have been arrested for that stunt, right?"

"Yes, they finally were," Sunny admitted.

"So, my ma and my aunt are currently in jail?" Those two wouldn't last an hour.

Sunny swiped a hand in front of her. "No, no. Your pop bailed them out and bought the parasailing company a whole new boat so they wouldn't press charges."

I blew out a relieved breath. "Like I always say, I live in the twilight zone."

"And your pop is a saint by the sounds of it."

"Cheers to that." We sipped. "This vacation was supposed to be an escape from my big, fat, crazy life. So much for that."

"Well, don't feel so bad." Sunny sighed. "Granny Gert just informed me that my six-month-old son who obviously can't talk yet just spoke to his great, great-grandmother. Try explaining *that* to his father."

~

Sunny

"How about you join us for some meditation this morning." Dallas the fitness director jerked his head in Mitch's direction. "Me thinks that someone looks like he could use a little relaxation, if you ask me."

"How about I help *you* get *your* head on straight." Mitch clenched his fists. "*Me* thinks that sounds like a dandy idea."

"It's okay, Dallas. It would take way more than one session to get Detective Grumpy Pants to relax." I glared at Mitch.

Dallas raised his hands up before him and slowly backed away. "I tried, honey," he said to me, then joined Simon Starks, the former excursion coordinator, by the pool getting the event ready.

"Cute, Tink," Mitch said dryly.

"Well, it's true. Ever since I told you about River communicating with Granny Gert's mother, you've been on edge." I stroked his whiskered cheek. "I love you, my darling, and I know you love me. I'm psychic, Mitch. It was bound to happen that at least one of our children would be as well. The old woman at the psychic fair told me as much."

"I know." He let out a big sigh. "Please don't think I won't love our son just as much as I love our daughter. It's just going to take some getting used to. Same that it took me a while to get used to *your* abilities. He's only six months old."

"Which means he's even more powerful than me," I pointed out.

Mitch's face paled. "And that scares the hell out of me. How will he ever relate to boring ole me?"

"You could never be boring." I kissed my husband firmly on the mouth. "He will relate to you because you're an amazing man and a wonderful father. But let's not dwell on that now. We have a murder to solve, remember?"

"Now *that*, I understand."

"Good." I looked over by the Java Junction coffee bar. Kalli and Nik were headed our way with our orders. But what interested me was the couple behind them. "Well, would you look at that?"

"What?" Mitch followed my gaze.

"Maria Giovanni is getting coffee with Roger Renegade, the security guard. What do you make of that?"

Mitch shrugged. "Not much. They're around the same age with a lot in common, apparently. He used to be in security before he retired, and now he spends his time as security on cruise ships. Says he loves to travel, and this is the best way. He offered to show Maria around the ship, and she took him up on it."

"That's sweet."

"He keeps saying the ship is haunted."

"I heard him say that as well. And I'm beginning to wonder if he's right." I looked back at Mitch. "I've had a bad feeling in my gut since we boarded this ship."

"Look who we found," Kalli said as she and Nik came to a stop by our table and handed us our coffee and tea.

Maria and Roger came up behind them and took the extra seats at our table.

"Good to officially meet you, Detective." Roger nodded once. "Captain Hughes informed me you two would be joining our team in the investigation."

Mitch shook his hand. "Name's Mitch. Good to meet you as well. I hear you've been on this ship for a while now."

He nodded. "Years. Never had something like this happen, though."

"Well, you're not alone. I've heard the stories, but I never imagined I would sail through the Bermuda Triangle and live to tell about it," I said.

"Me, either," Maria chimed in wistfully. "Dante would have been thrilled. He loved a good adventure."

Roger patted her hand. "I have to say I sense a strong energy on board. That was why I was so drawn to Maria, here." He smiled at her. "I truly feel her Dante is experiencing this cruise right along with her."

She beamed up at him.

"Oh, are you a psychic, too?" Nik asked.

"No, I'm an empath. I sense energies and feelings, but I haven't tapped into the ability on how to predict the future or read the past like you." He looked at me. "Your show was a big hit. Now everyone wants a reading."

"Well, I'm technically not supposed to be working."

Mitch grunted.

He wasn't technically supposed to be working, either. I ignored him and continued talking to Roger. "Many people have different levels of awareness. They just have to learn to develop that sixth sense. I bet you could get there if you worked at it."

His eyes grew wide. "I'm not sure I want to. The whole thing kind of freaks me out. That full-fledged psychic thing comes with a whole lot of baggage I'm not sure I'm ready for." He shook his head.

I could relate.

Mitch coughed but didn't say a word.

Smart man.

"But I definitely feel a larger-than-life presence," Roger continued.

"That would be my Dante." Maria beamed.

Roger's smile slipped, and he scratched his gray hair. "I also feel an overwhelming sense of doom. Like something big is coming, and it's not going to be good."

"Yes!" I surged to my feet and pumped the air, feeling validated. "I mean, I feel that, too." I sat back down. "I'm not sure what is going to happen, but I feel like Baron's murder is just the tip of the iceberg."

"You're really going to make a Titanic reference while we're stuck on a ship in the middle of the ocean?" Mitch raised a brow at me.

"Relax, honey." I patted his arm. "We're not going to sink."

"If Ma and Aunt Tasoula manage to sneak on board, we just might." Kalli blew out a breath, snapped her Barbie straw into shape, and took a tentative sip of slightly cooled tea.

"What are you talking about?" Nik gaped at her.

She held up her hand. "It's a whole other thing, hon. I didn't bring it up last night because I just can't deal with it. Let's just hope they've learned their lesson and stop being crazy."

"All I know is things can't get any crazier than they already are," Nik responded.

"Wanna bet?" Roger said.

And just like that, the power went out.

12

KALLI

"**O**h, my Zeus! It's happening," I blurted, every cell in my being filled with adrenaline as I surged to my feet. "Grab your life jackets, kiss your loved ones goodbye, we're going down like the Titanic." My fear of drowning getting the best of me.

"Calm down, Ballas," Nik whispered in my ear after he tugged me back down to my chair. "You're going to cause a panic."

"We *should* all panic!" He grabbed my hand before I could bolt and slipped his arm around me "We're about to be fish bait. I can't end up in Davey Jones's locker. Imagine the germs. I've seen Pirates of the Caribbean. They're all disgusting." I raised a brow. "Well, maybe not Captain Jack Sparrow."

I'm surprised you didn't say Will Turner. Nik arched a brow.

"Yes, him too, but still." I swiped my hand through the air, feeling the anxiety build in my stomach. "Never mind all that. The ocean is so dirty, I just can't spend eternity down there. I won't survive."

Of course not. You'd be dead. He quirked a brow.

"You're not helping."

"What? I didn't say a word." He grinned.

"Not funny." I felt the start of a panic attack coming on.

"Okay, okay, I'm sorry. Listen to reason. We're not in the Caribbean," he said gently. "We're halfway between Bermuda and New York City." *We're going to be okay, hon. I would never let anything happen to you.*

"I-I'll make room for you on the door, J-Jack." My voice hitched, and my eyes welled up with tears. "I-I'll save you."

Nik chuckled softly. "Again, this is not the Titanic, I'm not Leonardo DiCaprio, and no one is going to freeze to death." His eyes gentled as he pulled me onto his lap and held me in his arms. "But I appreciate you being my hero." He kissed me.

No sooner did the zip of current flow through me from Nik's kiss, dousing my anxiety, than the lights came back on.

I took a deep shaky breath.

"You good now?" He dipped his head to look me in the eyes.

I nodded, focusing on the warmth of his arms and the smell of his earthy cologne. It grounded me. He was my anchor. He was good for me in ways he'd never imagine. "I'm okay thanks to you."

Well, thanks to you, I'm great. He gave me a squeeze before letting go.

Meanwhile, in all the chaos, it looked like Sunny and Roger were having their own meltdowns.

"It's the ghost, I tell you." Roger shook his head and looked at Maria. "This ship is haunted. I'm certain of it."

Maria's eyes filled with fear. "You really think so?"

"I'm sensing an evil presence as well. I'm not sure if the entity is dead or alive. I keep feeling eyes burning a hole into my back, watching me. It's starting to freak me out." Sunny wrung her hands together.

Mitch's head was on a swivel, his body poised and alert. "You can damn sure bet I'll not let anything happen to the mother of my children." A muscle in his jaw clenched, and his intense gray eyes were more intimidating than the Devil's Triangle for anyone who didn't know him. "Don't you worry, Tink. They'll have to go through me to get to you."

Captain Hughes appeared on the Sky Deck stage with First Officer Tyrone Johnson and Chief Security Officer Justin Cho.

Diana handed her a microphone.

"Good morning, passengers. This is your captain speaking. There's no need to become alarmed. We're experiencing a simple power outage. We've had some technical malfunctions, but our engineering department is currently working to diagnose and address the situation as we speak. They are trained to handle technical issues related to the ship's systems, including power generation and distribution. They will work at implementing any necessary repairs or adjustments needed to restore power as quickly as possible."

Tyrone answered his phone and then leaned over and whispered something in the captain's ear. She nodded and continued speaking while he left the deck.

"In the meantime, we are equipped with backup generators that are up and running, as you can see. These generators are designed to ensure essential systems like navigation, lighting and safety equipment continue to function until the main power source is restored." She looked up at the sky. "It's a beautiful day, folks. Enjoy the rest of your time on board and thank you for your patience while we continue our investigation."

The captain handed the microphone back to Diana then walked off with PI Eddie and Agent Amy.

"You heard the captain, folks," Diana said with a cheery voice, pointing over to the pool. "Dallas and Simon are ready to show you all a great time with water aerobics, so come on up and join in the fun."

Cara started clapping loudly.

Diana scowled and left the stage.

"Well, I'm not on duty until this afternoon." Roger held out his arm. "Care to join me for a walk and enjoy this fine weather like the captain said?" He smiled at Maria, and I was pretty certain he was smitten with her.

Maria's cheeks flushed pink. "Why, that sounds like a lovely idea." She looped her arm through his, and they walked off together.

"What do you guys think we should do next?" I asked.

"Well, let's go over what we have so far." Sunny pulled out her notebook and flipped through the pages. "Crispin confirmed Baron's watch was a fake, yet Elton swears another watch that Baron wore earlier was the real deal. Why would Baron have a fake anything if he had the kind of money he said he did? And why was the fake in the lifeboat where the scene of the crime happened?" She tapped her notebook. "What I really want to know is what did Baron want to fix, and what wasn't fair to his daughter, Gracie?"

"All great questions." I had a few questions of my own. "Speaking of Gracie, why did Baron keep her a secret? Who did she tell what she knew and what did she actually know? Also, who was right all along that she didn't listen to, and what were they right about? She seemed worried she was in danger somehow."

"Exactly. I wonder if that's tied to the missing piece of art," Nik said. "Where did Baron hide it, and is it still there, or did someone find it and take it?"

"And I wonder what kind of enemies Baron might have had. Like Simon Stark, for example." Sunny looked over at the man gyrating in the pool.

My gaze followed hers. Simon moved like Pee Wee Herman next to Dallas who was clearly the next Richard Simmons, but hey, at least Diana had given him a job.

"Baron made it clear in Bermuda that Simon didn't like him," Sunny continued. "I mean, he went so far as to kick their entire group off an excursion."

"That's not surprising," I said. "Simon is a big environmental activist, and Baron had no respect for the earth or what he threw on it."

"Baron had no respect for a lot of things," Nik said. "It was clear he rubbed Milton the wrong way. Milton is still in good shape and passionate about old school money versus fake imitations. Maybe he killed him in a fit of rage." Nik shrugged. "I've seen even the most mellow person snap before when pushed too far."

"Something is definitely off with him." Mitch nodded. "He says he's from old money, yet he doesn't act like a man with no worries. I definitely think he has a gambling problem. He goes on all sorts of trips, yet his wife's family heirloom brooch is a fake. The kicker is she knows about it yet won't admit it. It's obviously eating her up inside to the point of affecting her health. She had a heart attack, for crying out loud. I'll follow up with my colleague and see if he found anything that explains their current lifestyle." Mitch pulled out his notebook and jotted down a note.

"We can't forget about Frankie," I interjected. "I knew he was a ladies' man, but who knew he was married with children. Courtney does *not* seem like a fan of his. Why is he spending so much time with Baron's daughter, Gracie? He clearly has many women, and she's so young. She doesn't seem his type. Why her?"

"Speaking of a ladies' man," Sunny added. "Frankie isn't the only man spending time with Gracie. Lance has made the rounds himself and seems *very* interested in Gracie as well. Did Chee Chee get jealous of Gracie and kill her father to get back at her? Or maybe Natalia did. She can't seem to let go of Lance."

"We all know she's obviously capable of devious acts to get back at someone." I ran a hand over my green chignon. "Then there's Ivan. He's so in love with her, I think he would do anything for her, and he's made it clear he despises Lance."

"You would be surprised what people are capable of when pushed hard enough," Nik said. "No one is off limits in my book."

"I agree." Mitch nodded. "What about Cara? She was in charge of the art auction. She seemed pretty chummy with Baron before he died. Was she trying to find out where he hid the prized piece of art? And what is up with the feud between her and Diana? Diana seemed adamant that the art auction be shut down. Why? Maybe Diana had a thing for Baron and was jealous of Cara."

Sunny was already shaking her head. "That's not it."

"How can you be so sure?" Mitch asked.

"Let's just say I've *seen* where her desire truly lies," Sunny responded. "And that's all I'm going to say about that."

Mitch's eyes widened with understanding. Sunny

didn't need to break her promise for the truth to become clear....

Captain Heather Hughes's secret affair was with cruise director Diana North.

~

Sunny

"Are you sure we're allowed to do this?" Kalli asked.

We came to a stop outside of Baron's room. There was still crime scene tape around it. With the lifeboat gone, the only possible evidence left regarding Baron's murder would be in the room he had occupied. That is where the struggle with the killer started before Baron ran off and the killer followed him to the lifeboat.

"Yes, we can do this," I said adamantly. "Captain Hughes gave us free reign. Besides, she and her team are all occupied with briefing Mitch and Nik, so it's all good. I say we take advantage of the freedom to explore the room fully without watchful eyes. Maybe we can find out where Baron hid the art."

"Excuse me," said an older man of around fifty with a room steward uniform on as he approached us with a frown. "Can I help you?"

Every guest on board had a medallion with their photo and personal information stored digitally on it. Then the medallion was inserted into a necklace or wrist band or clip to be worn by the passenger. It served as their wallet, their ID to get on and off the ship, and their room key. The door unlocked automatically but only for the guests registered to that room.

Room Stewards, however, had a master key for their entire floor.

I looked at his badge. "Joe Baxter, it's nice to meet you." I held out my hand.

He shook it warily. "And you are?"

"Forgive my manners. My name is Sunshine Meadows Stone, but you can call me Sunny. Everybody does."

His eyes widened. "You're that psychic." His gaze settled on Kalli in awe. "And you must be her sidekick." He snapped his fingers. "Mystical Mavens."

"That's me." She shook his hand and held on. "I make a great assistant, and we're hoping you can assist us."

He looked deep in thought for a moment. "Well, I'm not sure—"

"The answer's yes." Kalli dropped his hand. "Sunny would be happy to give you a reading."

He sucked in a sharp breath. "How'd you know I was thinking that?"

"Mystical Mavens, remember?" She winked. "I do a little more than assist from time to time."

"Kalli's right. If you could assist us into this room, I would be happy to give you a reading after." I smiled wide at him.

"Oh, I don't want no trouble, ma'am."

"There won't be any trouble, I promise you. In fact, *we* are assisting the captain in investigating Baron's murder."

"Maybe I should call—"

"That won't be necessary. The captain is in a meeting with her team and our men. They're detectives and helping out as well." I took his arm and encouraged him to walk with me to the door. "So, about that reading? The sooner you let us in, the quicker I'll be able to see into your future."

Excitement shimmered in his eyes. "Well, I suppose it wouldn't hurt to let you look around. That FBI lady and Belgian private investigator guy have already been over every inch of this room, so I imagine they found whatever they're going to."

"Exactly," Kalli said with encouragement.

Joe let us into Baron's room, and an eerie feeling swept over me. I could feel a heaviness in the air. It was almost as if Baron's spirit couldn't rest until his murder was solved. Like he was still carrying a lot of weight around. I felt the anger, frustration, and resentment of a life taken too soon. He had burdens left to take care of...

And he wanted me to take care of them for him.

I inhaled a long, slow breath and looked around the room. *I'm working on it, but you've got to back off and give me space. Now, go away.* The heaviness lifted, and suddenly, I could breathe again.

"Sunny, I said are you okay?" Kalli searched my eyes. "You got really pale all of a sudden."

I blinked. "I'm better now."

The room was a large suite, even bigger than ours or Kalli and Nik's. There wasn't an inch of the room that wasn't trashed, as if someone had been looking for something in particular. Baron must have discovered the person in the act because items were broken as if from a fight.

I had to focus if I was going to be able to read anything this time.

"So, tell me, Joe, did a lot of people come and go from Baron's room?" Kalli asked, giving me time to pull myself together.

Joe shrugged. "A lot of women, and one young one."

Kalli looked at me. *Gracie.*

"They argued a lot," he went on. "Got a few calls

from other cabins about them disturbing the peace. I heard them a few times myself. It wasn't that difficult because they were so loud."

"Really? What did they argue about?" I asked.

"Money," he said. "She wasn't happy that he kept her hidden. He had the nicer room. He didn't give her enough of an allowance. That kind of stuff. She seemed way too young for him if you ask me, but who am I to judge."

Joe clearly didn't know she was his daughter, I thought.

"Anything else?" Kalli asked.

"He did tell her once that he couldn't let them find out about her, or they would use her to get to him. Whatever that meant." Joe held up his hands. "She didn't seem to believe him because she defied him anyway from what I could tell. Then after he died, she did come back to the room one time. I heard her crying, saying she should have listened to him. That he had been right all along and now it was too late."

"Thank you, Joe." Kalli rested her hand on his shoulder. "You've been a big help to us. And yes, Sunny can do that reading for you now so you can clean the rest of the rooms on this floor."

He blinked and his lips parted.

She winked and moved her hand from his shoulder.

"Have a seat, Joe, and take my hands." I sat in a chair.

He sat on the couch, facing me.

I took his hands in my own and closed my eyes in concentration. "I see a bright future for you, Joe. Life is going to get better for you, my friend. You're going to get a promotion and be able to help your family back home."

I felt him breathe a sigh of relief. He started to let go of my hands.

"Wait, there's more." I refocused and suddenly the past came into vision.

I saw him cleaning this room many times, swaying to Frank Sinatra as he did so. A hint of a smile tipped up the corners of my lips. Joe was very thorough, making impressive animals out of towels and leaving them on the bed with chocolates. He treated his guests well. My smile faded. Baron was a slob. I saw every part of the suite, and suddenly, something stuck out to me. I opened my eyes and abruptly stood, walking over to the corner bar that faced the whole living room and door.

"Where's the little teddy bear that was sitting right here." I touched the table and looked at Joe.

"I don't know," he said. "It was gone after Mr. Von Wielig was murdered." He stood. "If that's all, I really have to finish my shift before the guests return."

"That's all." I smiled. "And thank you."

He nodded and held the door open for us to leave. "Thank *you*. I can rest a little easier now." The door locked itself as we all left.

He headed down the hall with lighter steps, and we headed in the opposite direction. We rounded a corner and saw Chee Chee and Lance walking arm-in-arm together, her head resting against his shoulder all intimate like.

"Looks like Mr. Magic got his assistant back," Kalli said with a scoff. "Better her than me." She looked back at me after they disappeared around another corner. "What was so special about that teddy bear, anyway?"

I shook my head. "Not just a teddy bear." I looked around to make sure we were alone. "Baron had a nanny cam. I predict the killer's image is recorded on it."

"The question is who has it now?"

"Exactly. It has to be on this ship somewhere."

Kalli studied me with a sparkle of excitement in her eyes. "I don't have to read your mind to know what you're thinking."

I rubbed my hands together. "We find that nanny cam, we find our killer."

13

KALLI

"Thank you for accommodating us, Xavier," Officer Roger said to our head waiter as he pulled out Maria's chair at our table in the Maritime Eatery dining room later that evening. Then he took the seat beside her.

Baron's old seat.

Xavier tipped his bald head to the side and pushed his glasses further up his nose. "My pleasure, Roger. Thank goodness the power is fully restored. I'm just glad Ms. Giovanni has a great guy like you to keep her company. She's a fine lady."

"I couldn't agree more. I like dining with Chief Security Officer Justin just fine, but Ms. Maria here is about the loveliest dinner companion I've ever had." Roger's eyes lit up when he looked at her.

Maria had told us Roger had never married. He'd simply never had time and never met anyone who made him want to find the time. A positive aura and good energy was important to him, and Maria embodied both of those.

Her beloved Dante had been gone a year now. This cruise was about saying goodbye to him and celebrating a great love. Milton and Mavis were celebrating an old love. While Sunny and Mitch and Nik and me were celebrating new loves.

Maybe this was the love boat after all.

Maria blushed. "Well, my word. You gentlemen sure are full of flattery." She patted her perfectly curled and set dark head of hair.

"I'm simply speaking the truth." Roger smiled.

Xavier set our menus in front of us. "We have baked Alaska tonight. Let me know when you're ready to order." He tipped his head and then walked away.

Roger looked around the room. "The energy is good in here tonight for a change."

"I agree," Sunny said, looking relieved. "It will be nice to eat in peace."

We all remained silent over the mention of negative energy. I had seen how it affected Sunny, and it had unnerved me as well. Reading minds was one thing, but I was no Ghostbuster. I focused on tonight's menu, but it didn't really matter. The cook knew by now to prepare a special meal just for me. It turned out he had a daughter just like me and didn't mind catering to my special needs one bit.

That warmed my heart.

Xavier returned and everyone else placed their orders.

"How are you feeling, Mavis?" I asked her after our waiter left. She looked a little pale. I noticed she no longer wore her brooch. I didn't dare ask her about it because she seemed a little fragile at the moment.

"I'm okay, dear. Just a little tired." She smiled.

"Dr. Chopra said she needs some fancy procedure, but I'm getting a second opinion when we get home. I'll spare no expense, mind you, but with the doctor of my choice. We have the best doctors in Boston, don't we, lovie?" Milton squeezed her hand.

Her smile slipped a little, but she nodded. "I'll be fine, I'm sure. It's nothing that can't wait until we get home. No need to go crazy right now. Let's just make the best of our time left until they let us go." She patted his hand.

Xavier approached Milton and spoke quietly before slipping away.

Milton frowned then looked at us. "Excuse me. There's a matter I must attend to." He whispered something to Mavis, then stood and walked out of the dining room without another word.

Mavis paled even more. "Excuse me as well. I'm suddenly not hungry anymore. I think I'll go lie down for a spell."

"I wonder what that was all about," I said.

Nik and Mitch looked at each other.

"I'm not a betting man, but I'm pretty sure it has to do with the bill he's racked up in the casino," Nik said. "The other day, another one of his cards was declined while Mitch and I were there."

Mitch nodded. "During our meeting with the captain today, I got a call from my buddy who was looking into Milton. It turns out he *is* from old money, but he's broke. He loses as much as he wins."

Nik sighed. "Yeah, we're pretty sure he pawned his wife's family heirloom because of his gambling addiction."

"Oh, no," I said. "Poor Mavis. No wonder she doesn't look good."

"If Milton and Mavis are broke, then how do they keep affording to go on all of these trips?" Sunny asked.

"That is the million-dollar question," Mitch said.

"Baron had money," Roger chimed in. "Desperate people are capable of all sorts of things. Milton clearly didn't like Baron from what I could tell. Maybe he broke into his room, hoping to find something of value, but Baron caught him in the act. It could happen. Just saying it's food for thought."

"Speaking of food, ours is here," Maria said. "I'm starving. Let's eat. And then maybe we can go to the show. I hear Angela is performing better than ever."

"Better than Elton?" Roger raised a brow.

Maria shrugged. "Let's just say something...or someone...has put a pep in her step as of late."

I wondered if a certain art enthusiast with white and gold hair had something to do with her improvement. Only one way to find out. "Count me in."

~

Sunny

"It sure is nice being on the other side of the entertainment, isn't it?" I sat beside Kalli in Poseidon's Palace theater.

"You aren't kidding." She shuddered, sinking down into the plush comfort of her seat. "I hate being in the spotlight, and I will never go into a box of any kind again, not even when I die. At least with cremation, all the germs will burn up. Wood rots and bugs live beneath the ground. No thank you."

I laughed. "You crack me up, girlfriend." A movement over by the side of the stage by the edge of the curtain caught my eye, and I tapped Kalli's arm. "Hey, isn't that Natalia with Chee Chee?"

Kalli turned her head in that direction and squinted. "It sure looks that way. And they don't look very happy."

I gasped and sat up straighter. "Did you see that? It looked like Natalia just shoved Chee Chee?"

"Yes, she most certainly did. And look." Kalli sat up straighter as well and pointed. "There's Ivan. Oh boy, he just took Natalia by the arm and escorted her off the stage. I wonder where Lance is?"

"I saw him out in the lobby with Gracie earlier," I said. "That can't be good."

"My heart goes out to Natalia." Kalli shook her head, her hair almost fully back to its natural blond now. "Why can't she just forget about Lance? He's clearly not good for her mental health."

"And where does Gracie fit into all of this I wonder?"

"Who knows." Kalli stood up and waved. "There's Nik and Mitch, just in time for the show."

The lights dimmed just as they reached our seats.

"Here you go." Nik handed Kalli a glass of chardonnay.

"Thank you." She set her drink on the tray table attached to our oversized seats. The VIP section came as part of our package deal. She snapped her straw together and handed me a matching spare.

Mitch handed me a fuzzy naval then sat down.

"Looks yummy." I snapped the straw she'd given me together and slipped it into the glass then took a big sip and sighed in delight.

Roger and Maria sat further down from us as the curtains pulled back. For the next hour, Elton and Angela put on quite the show with background singers, amazing dancers with flashy costumes, and a light show worthy of Vegas. Elton had an amazing voice, but Angela shined the brightest tonight. Something seemed different about her.

It was like the energy from her early days as a star had filled her once more.

I noticed a white and gold head of hair sitting in the front row, swaying to the music, and singing along. Rafe Overton. I did a double take. Gracie was sitting beside him, and Lance was nowhere in sight. What did that mean?

The curtains closed, and everyone gave a standing ovation as the lights came back on.

"Let's make our way over for an autograph," Maria said. "I've always been a big fan of Angela's."

We all followed her to the stage as the theater emptied out.

Angela and Elton signed autographs, but Angela's line was longer. Elton didn't look pleased about that. Mitch and Nik went over to talk to him while Kalli and I stood in line to officially meet Angela.

"Sunny, it's good to see you again," Rafe said with a smile. "Have you got your sea legs yet?"

"Oh, yes. And it's only my first cruise."

"I remember my first cruise years ago. I predict you'll come to love cruising." He laughed. "I sure do. I saw your show. I didn't realize you were so talented. You and your sidekick there." He gestured to Kalli.

"Sidekick Sister at your service." Kalli saluted him, then looked pensive. "You love cruising? But I thought in the store in Bermuda you said this was your first cruise."

His smile slipped a hair then widened, revealing a row of white capped perfect teeth. "I meant this is my first cruise on this line of ships."

"My mistake." She shrugged.

"This cruise hasn't turned out like I had expected it to, given a murder happened, but I have to say it's not *all* bad." He looked at Angela and winked.

"Good for you," I said. "You seem a lot more confident than when we first met you on the island."

"I've always been confident. I must have had a moment of weakness the first time you met me." He brushed a hand over the sleeve of his jacket. "Many things inspire confidence in a man, Mrs. Stone. The finer things in life. A good woman. Money." He shrugged. "You would be surprised the lengths a man will go to impress a beautiful woman." He sighed. "If only work didn't keep getting in the way."

"Oh, I didn't know you were on board to work. You should take her to the art gallery," I said, assuming his work had to do with his love of art.

"Nah, I don't know anything about art, but I do know a thing or two about jewelry. Thanks for the idea."

"But—"

Angela walked over to us. "There you are, darling," she said to Rafe. "Who are your friends?"

"The infamous Mystical Mavens, Sunny Stone and Kalli Ballas." He gestured dramatically to us.

"It's a pleasure meeting you," Kalli said.

"You sounded wonderful," I added.

"Charmed, I'm sure. I saw your little act earlier. It was cute." She looked down her nose at us.

Suddenly, I was Team Elton.

Dismissing us, Angela looked back at Rafe. "I'm famished. Let's go eat."

"Right away. Think about what specialty restaurant you want to go to. I just need another word with Ms. Marks. I'll meet you at your dressing room in five minutes." He kissed her cheek and headed over to Gracie while Angela wandered backstage.

"What's that look on your face about?" Mitch asked as he and Nik joined us.

"A couple things." I studied Rafe as he finished his conversation with Gracie then made his way back-stage. "What business does Rafe Overton have with Baron's daughter? Also, he just said he didn't know anything about art and was more into jewelry."

"Yet when we first met him in Bermuda, he admired the art in the shop, claiming to be an art afi-cionado," Kalli added. "He's also way more confident now."

"I know," I said. "It's weird."

"You know what else is weird?" Nik asked.

"What." Kalli arched a brow at him.

"Chee Chee wears a blond wig," he replied.

"That's not so unusual," I said. "A lot of enter-tainers wear wigs."

"The watch you found in the lifeboat had a golden blond strand of hair stuck in the clasp," Mitch said. "Special Agent Randolph sent it to the lab, and they confirmed it was from a wig."

"That's not all," Nik said. "The CSI team found an-other hair of the same fibers in Baron's room."

"We need to find that nanny cam," I muttered.

"Wait...what?" Mitch narrowed his eyes at me.

I looked at Kalli and she nodded, so I turned to my husband to face the music with a sigh. "While you two were at your meeting with the captain and her team, we paid Baron's room steward a visit."

"Of course, you two did." Nik shook his head at Kalli.

"Just because you two are on the team now, doesn't mean that we are off." She crossed her arms over her chest.

"Never mind all that. It's not important. I found something." I looked at Mitch. "I had a vision. There was a teddy bear nanny cam in Baron's room when Joe last cleaned it, and now it's gone since the murder. Whoever killed him is most likely on that camera. We find that camera, we find our killer."

"And possibly the missing art," Mitch pointed out.

My cell rang through the app and I looked at the caller ID. "It's the captain."

"Why would she call you and not us?" Mitch frowned.

There was only one way to find out. "Sunny Stone, here. What can I do for you, Captain?" I listened to her speak. "Oh no, since when?" She spoke some more.

Mitch and Nik looked at the alarmed expression on my face and then at each other. They were on their feet, gathering our things in an instant.

"Okay, I'll tell the others." I hung up.

"What's wrong?" Kalli asked.

"The captain needs our help right away," I said to Kalli.

"Then let's go," Nik said.

"I still don't get why she would call you instead of us." Mitch gathered our things with a frown.

"Because this is a job for Mystical Mavens," I said carefully. "She needs our special abilities on this one."

"What happened?" Kalli asked.

"Cara Carmichael is missing."

14

KALLI

Horizon Harbor Art Deck consisted of a long hall with a thick plush beige carpet, filled from floor to ceiling with art in all shapes and sizes. I loved going to art galleries and seeing a rising star's exhibition or an already established artist's collection. Glorious masterpieces on easels and pedestals and along the wall beneath just the right lighting.

Spectacular.

Nik had never understood how people could pay so much money for and make such a fuss over someone else's idea of creativity. I told him it was all a matter of interpretation and expression. That if he kept an open mind and was willing to debate a piece, he might enjoy the experience better, but he had no interest in any of it. Sunny said Mitch was the same way, so it was probably a good thing the captain had called on us to get to the bottom of Cara's vanishing act.

Baron's client was a young woman by the name of Abigail Hernandez who had taken the art world by storm. She was a contemporary artist who produced dynamic works, using various concepts and methods as well as a variety of materials and subjects. Her works were influenced by a world full of diversity, advancements in technology, and global influences. Contemporary art appealed to me with the way it challenged boundaries by not conforming. Abigail's work dealt with her family and community and the influences her culture played in her life.

I, for one, was excited to meet her.

Brie and Haden were talking to Agent Amy and PI Eddie when Sunny and I approached them. A missing person fell under FBI jurisdiction, while Justin and his officers covered other security issues on board. Mitch and Nik were still looking into leads regarding Baron's murder investigation.

"Sunny." Eddie nodded his bald head once, his buff body at full attention. "Kalli." He nodded to me as well, his square jaw rigid and lips in a firm line. The man was all business and more intimidating than Mitch.

"Oh, good, you're both here." Amy nodded her fiery head of red hair. "I'm hoping maybe you can pick up some clues while in here. We were just talking to the photographers, and they said it's very unusual for Cara not to show up for her shift."

Brie stood as tall and fit as Amy, with her jet-black hair in a high ponytail and a clipboard in her hands. "Ms. Carmichael is never late for an event, especially with Mr. Von Wielig gone. She finally got the okay from the captain to have the auction, even without the prized piece of art." Brie shook her head. "She wouldn't have missed this."

Haden wore his dark blond hair in his usual manbun with a camera around his neck, stroking his tight clipped beard. "We got to know Cara during this trip. She's not just an auctioneer. She knows a lot about art and cares about artists. She and Abigail have become close. No one has seen Cara since the power went out and she argued with the cruise director on the Sky Deck."

"The show must go on as they say," Brie added, "so Diana is on her way to cover the event. It's supposed to start in thirty minutes. People will be arriving soon." She looked across the room at a young woman fixing the art displays. "Poor Abigail is a mess. Can't say that I blame her. This is her career we're talking about. A piece of her art is missing, and her auction is in jeopardy of not happening."

"We'll go talk to her and look around." Sunny scanned the room. "Maybe we'll get a reading off something."

"Good," Eddie said just as Diana entered the hallway. "I'll handle Ms. North." He took long, purposeful strides in her direction.

Amy rolled her eyes. "Men. They always think they're in charge." She shook her head. "No matter how high I climb that ladder, I still have to prove myself." She sighed. "Let me know if you find anything." We nodded, and she walked away with just as long purposeful strides to join Eddie and Diana.

"Come on. Let's go talk to Abigail." I turned in her direction with Sunny by my side. "I'm a big fan of her work."

"Me, too. Those statues are gorgeous, and the paintings are stunning." Sunny looked around in awe. "Her use of color is amazing."

"Finally, someone who appreciates art like I do."

"Abigail Hernandez?" Sunny came to a stop beside the young woman.

The petite woman with short, curly dark hair spun

around with wide amber eyes. She placed a hand on her chest. "Oh, my, you startled me."

"Sorry, I didn't mean to frighten you. My name is Sunny, and this is my friend, Kalli." Sunny pointed at me.

"I'm a huge fan of your work." I held out my hand. "It's such a pleasure to meet you."

Abigail relaxed and shook my hand, smiling a little sadly. "Thank you so much. That means a lot to me. My career has taken off so quickly, it's all a little overwhelming." *I can't do this alone.*

"Oh, I predict you'll do just fine." I let go of her hand.

She blinked and looked at me confused.

"We're working with the FBI as consultants on Baron Von Wielig's murder investigation and Cara Carmichael's disappearance," Sunny chimed in. "Is there anything you can tell us that might help?"

"I'm not sure." Abigail looked pensive. "I was so excited when Mr. Von Wielig booked this cruise for us. He told me it would be great exposure for my work internationally, and that I needed to relax and have fun. Then someone murdered him." She folded her arms across her chest. "I just don't understand who would want to kill him."

"So, you don't know of any enemies he might have had?" Sunny asked.

"He was a great businessman, and he sure knew a lot about art. I respected that about him, but he tended to rub a lot of people the wrong way. The easier question might be who *wasn't* his enemy?" Abigail lifted a shoulder.

"Did you know he had a daughter about your age?" I asked.

She frowned. "He told me he didn't have any family."

"That's what he told everyone," Sunny said. "Her name is Gracie, and she's on board this ship."

"That was his daughter?" Abigail sputtered. "I had no idea. I saw them together a lot, often arguing. But he spent time with many women of all ages, so I didn't think anything of it." She nodded. "She's Hispanic like me. He's not, so she must get that from her mother's side. I wonder if that's why he offered to help me."

"I don't know about that," I said. "You're definitely not a charity case. Your work is in high demand." I looked around. "Your pieces speak to people. It's all about connecting with others, and you do that well with your art."

"Well, thank you. I work so hard on these pieces, putting my heart and soul into them." She brushed away a tear. "For a prized piece from my collection to go missing is heartbreaking. I never should have let it out of my sight."

"I know it's supposed to be a secret, but can you tell us what the missing piece is and what it looks like?" I glanced around at some smaller pieces I had decided I wanted to bid on. They would look wonderful in our home, once Nik and I knocked down that final wall. *Our home.* The thought filled me with more joy and love than I'd ever allowed myself to imagine I could have.

"It's a mosaic sculpture of a pair of dolphins made from sea glass. There are tiny fairy lights inside that make the colors of the glass glow when they are lit. I just…I feel like someone stole a part of me. I'm so stressed it's still missing." Abigail swallowed the slight crackle in her voice.

"Speaking of missing things." Sunny shot a look at

me that said she'd read *my* mind. "Do you know anything about Cara Carmichael's disappearance?"

Abigail was already shaking her head. "No. We became friends during this cruise, especially after the murder. Cara has been there every step of the way for me, unlike a certain someone who's tried to ruin everything." Her gaze shot over to Amy, Eddie, and Diana who were still deep in conversation. "I find it rather coincidental that the minute Cara got the approval to go ahead with the auction, she winds up missing. Now, Diana is suddenly in charge." Abigail sighed. "She found a way to get exactly what she wanted after all."

"Do you mind if we touch a few of your pieces?" Sunny asked. "I'd like to see if I can get a reading on what might have happened to Cara."

Abigail sucked in a breath. "You're the Mystical Mavens. I don't know how I missed that. Can you read me? Actually, wait. I'd rather not know. I can't take any more disappointment this week. Feel free to read anything else, though."

"Thank you," I said. "We'll let you know if we find anything."

For the next half hour, Sunny and I wandered around, touching pieces of Abigail's work to no avail. We had just made our way back up front as the auction was about to start.

"Well, at least we tried." Sunny picked up Cara's gavel.

Her head snapped back, and she looked as if she was in a trance. I knew enough by now not to interrupt her when she had a vision. Eddie and Amy joined us, and I held up a finger to shush them. They both looked a little unnerved but remained silent.

"I'm going to need that gavel," Diana suddenly said from behind us.

Sunny snapped out of her trance and blinked.

"What's wrong with her?" Diana stepped back with a wary frown.

Ignoring her, I asked, "Sunny, are you okay?"

"It was dark and stuffy, and I felt so seasick," she said quietly.

"What does that mean?" Eddie asked.

Sunny looked at him. "Cara Carmichael is still on board this ship." She looked at Amy as she finished with, "and she's still very much alive."

~

Sunny

We searched the entire ship for Cara Carmichael with no luck. I felt helpless, and my energy was sapped. Visions tended to do that to me. Kalli's hands were getting chapped from rubbing so much hand sanitizer on them after shaking so many hands and touching people, trying to hear something useful.

We both needed a break.

Mitch and Nik were still following their own leads, but they suggested we do something fun together to clear our minds. This was supposed to be our vacation, after all. But I was a bit shocked when they suggested we go to Knockin' Boots. It was the country-western bar with bull riding, the Texas Two-Step, and country line dances like the Tush Push, the West Coast Shuffle, the Redneck Girl, and the Boot Scootin' Boogie.

"This was such a great idea." I slid onto a bar stool next to Kalli.

Mitch was to my left and Nik was to her right. We wore fun sundresses and had found some cowboy boots and hats in one of the shops. The men had even played along with jeans, button down shirts, boots, and hats. I was shocked when Nik talked Mitch into a hat, but I think he knew this trip hadn't turned out like any of us had planned.

So, he was being a good sport, and playing along just to make me happy. Not to mention, he looked darn good in a Stetson.

"I agree," Kalli said. "We needed the break."

"What can I get for you all?" Frankie looked a little flustered. He flipped his sandy brown bangs to the side and studied us with distracted hazel eyes, the charmer in him all but gone.

"How about something different," I said. "I'll have a margarita."

"You know what? I'll have the same." Kalli nodded.

"Well, all right then. Let's go with a Corona for me." Nik slapped the smooth mahogany bar.

"Make mine a Modello." Mitch ordered with a nod of his head.

"Coming right up." Frankie slid down the bar to make the drinks.

Courtney joined us, placing a couple bowls of cocktail peanuts before us. "Hi, ladies. Are you ready to join in the fun?"

I clapped my hands. "Of course."

"Um, I tried a new drink." Kalli eyed the nuts the men were diving into and looked a little ill. "I think that's enough for one night. It's a known fact that most people don't wash their hands after using the bathroom."

Courtney laughed. "Okay, so no bar food. But how

about dancing? You don't even have to touch anyone so no germs."

"What if someone sneezes?" Kalli held up a finger. "Germs can travel up to six feet in the air from a single sneeze."

"Come on. Live a little. You can't miss out on all the fun by worrying about everything." Courtney looked at the stage and the light reflected off her nose ring. "You know Dallas and Simon won't let you get away with that."

"That's what I'm afraid of," Kalli muttered.

"It's busy in here tonight," I said.

"Nothing else to do during lockdown." Courtney shrugged. "It's either the casino, the theater, or the bars in the evening."

"Frankie looks a little off his game," Kalli said.

Courtney snorted. "That's not because of the crowd. He thrives on that." She leaned in for our ears only. "He's unsettled because his wife just filed for divorce. She finely wised up and is leaving him." Her face hardened. "I hate cheaters. I hope she takes him for all he's worth, but you didn't hear the news from me."

Frankie made his way back to us with our drinks, and Courtney walked away to wait on more customers.

"There you go," he said.

Gracie walked in at that moment and headed for the bar.

"I think I'll take my break now," Frankie said. He spoke to another bartender and then intercepted Gracie, said something to her, then they both left the club.

I drew my eyebrows together then took a sip of my margarita. "For someone so young who just lost her father and is supposed to be in mourning, she sure does get around."

"No kidding." Kalli took a sip of her own drink. "I've seen her at all the events, and spending time with Lance, Rafe, and Frankie."

"Hey, ladies, no work." Nik wagged his finger at us.

"Yeah, you're supposed to be taking the night off." Mitch tipped back his longneck bottle and took a long pull from it.

"You're right." Kalli took another dainty sip.

"I thought you said you were done trying something new." I grinned.

"I am, why?" She looked at me curiously.

"You just drank directly from your glass a couple times with no straw in sight."

Kalli's lips parted and her face paled. "I did?"

"You sure did. And you lived to tell about it." I laughed. "Now come dance with me." I grabbed her hand and pulled her with me.

"That's right, folks," Dallas spoke into a microphone. "Don't be shy. Come on out to the dance floor." Instead of a fishing pole, he grabbed an imaginary rope this time and twirled it over his head then launched it in my direction.

I slapped my arms to my side as if I'd been lassoed.

He roared with laughter and pulled me to the dance floor.

"Oh, for the love of Poseidon, what did I get myself into?" Kalli kept her feet moving. "If he tries to rope me, I'll knock him off his saddle."

I giggled.

"Simon here is going to show you all how to do the moves. Heel close, heel close, heel, two, three." The crowd followed along. "Now bump your hip out twice and bump your hip twice again." People laughed and kept messing up, but everyone was having a good time. "Then single, two, three, four. That's right, folks. Right, left, right and rock. Left, right, left and rock. This is called the Tush Push, and I'm here if any of you need any help pushing your tushes." Dallas winked.

Mitch choked on his beer, grabbed his hat, and joined us with Nik hot on his heels.

Dallas's face lit up. He picked up his lasso and aimed it toward Mitch.

My husband let his hand hover over an imaginary holster and gave Dallas a look that said, *Don't go there, partner. I have backup.*

Nik stood by his side with an itchy trigger finger.

Dallas got the message. "Let's skip that dance for now, folks. Everyone loves a good Texas Two-Step." He signaled the band.

Slow music came on, but I couldn't complain as Mitch took me in his arms and moved me gracefully around the room in a big circle.

"Well, look at you, Mr. Stone." I stared up at him in wonder.

"I still have a few surprises up my sleeve, Mrs. Stone."

"This is more my speed, partner." Nik twirled Kalli alongside of us.

"Me, too." She laughed.

And just like that the party was over when Gracie Marks stumbled into the bar and collapsed in the middle of the dance floor.

15

KALLI

"**S**he's beaten up pretty good, but she'll live," Doctor Chopra said. "I'd like to keep her for observation."

"No." Gracie looked alarmed. "I don't want to stay here. You can't make me. I want to go back to my room now."

"We'll take her back to her room," I said.

Gracie had specifically gone to the country-western bar because she knew Sunny and I were there. She went there after she was attacked to find us, but then she passed out. After Mitch and Nik got her to the medical center, she came to and panicked. She wanted them to leave. She wanted everyone gone except for Sunny, me, and the doctor.

She wouldn't tell us what she and Frankie spoke about. All she said was that they talked for a little while, and then she went to the ladies' room. When she came out of the stall and was washing her hands, someone jumped her from behind. She never saw her attacker's face. They kept hitting her hard, over and over, then knocked her to the ground and left her for dead. She managed to get up and make it back into the club before passing out.

She supposedly had no idea who would want to do this to her.

Nik and Mitch went off to question Chee Chee. Amy said she'd take care of questioning Lance. And Eddie headed off to talk to Natalia. Frankie never came back from his break. Nik sent me a text. When they went to his room, he said he was in bed sick the whole time, but he didn't have anyone there to verify his alibi.

"I don't like the idea of letting you go back to your room alone, but I can't force you to stay here." Dr. Chopra handed Sunny a bottle of pills. "I gave her pain meds." The doctor looked at Gracie with a firm expression. "I want you to stay in your room and rest. Call me if you need anything at all." She handed her card to Gracie.

"Thank you, Dr. Chopra, I will." Gracie gingerly stood.

Sunny and I each took one of her arms and walked her out into the hall and to the elevator. *Why is my life so horrible? All I wanted was my father's attention. I feel so guilty. It's all my fault. What if I'm the reason he's dead?*

My gaze shot to Sunny's, and she arched a brow. Wait until I told her what I heard later. We reached Gracie's floor, finally. Her exhaustion was kicking in and her mind had been blank the rest of the trip. The hallway was empty.

"Do you have your medallion?" I asked her.

Her hand fluttered to her neck. "No. It's missing. I didn't even notice."

"Guys, look," Sunny said. "The door's ajar. Wait there while I check it out."

We stood back, and she pulled out...oh my Zeus, she pulled out the pink collapsible straw I had given her and snapped it together.

"Now, what on earth do you think that's going to do?" I arched a brow at her.

"Poke someone's eye out? I mean, it's metal." She shrugged. "It's better than nothing, right?"

"You really think I came on a cruise with nothing?" I opened my purse and pulled out a pen. "This lovely lady holds mace. Just click it, and the stream sprays out."

Sunny gaped at me. "How did you get that through security?"

I winked. "It's under three ounces."

She looked fascinated. "What else you got?"

I took off my shoe. "How about the knife in the toe of my shoe trick."

She gasped. "No way." Her eyebrows drew together. "Again, how did you get a blade through security?"

I tapped my toe and the blade slid out. "It's made of plastic, but hard plastic is just as effective to stab someone, especially if I kick hard enough."

Her eyebrows shot up. "Good lord, anything else?"

"You know those little red laser pointers that look like a pen? Well, I found these sunglasses that shoot out a laser beam when you push on the frames. They say to never shine a laser beam in someone's eyes. I figured it might come in handy one day."

Sunny shook her head. "You amaze me."

I snapped my fingers and pulled out my last item. "Oh, and I do have this special toothpaste."

"Let me guess. It explodes." She snorted.

"No, silly. That would be crazy and impossible to get through security. But I did mix the toothpaste with cayenne pepper and stored it in this less than three-ounce container." I grinned. "I figured I could use this for a number of things. Burn the eyes, scald the throat, grease a squeaky wheel."

"What?"

"Hey, you never know." I shrugged. "I come prepared for any possible situation when I travel."

"I can see that." She leaned forward to peer inside my purse. "Do you have a tiny Q in there?"

I wrinkled my nose. "What's a Q?"

"If you have to ask, then never mind." She laughed. "I'll take...you know what? Just give me the whole thing."

"Okay but be careful with Venus." I handed her the bag.

"Venus?"

"My purse. It used to be Ma's, remember? She thinks I'm silly for naming it." I shrugged. "Venus is another name for Aphrodite, which is the name of my parents' restaurant. She's the Greek goddess of love and beauty—all the things I'm inspired to be but didn't know I was capable of until I woke up with my gift and met Nik."

"I have no clue what you just said. It was beautiful, but we need to get moving." She took my purse and one of my shoes.

Tapping my shoe—which was way too big for her foot—onto her hand, the plastic blade popped out. She gripped it in her hand while slipping my purse over her shoulder. Carefully peeking around the corner, she pushed the door open and ran inside with her arms waving and shrieking like a banshee.

I was pretty sure that wasn't the way normal detectives did things, but I didn't want to be *that* girl. So, I stayed in place, holding up an exhausted Gracie, and waited for the *all clear*. Moments later, Sunny's voice rang out loud and clear and full of angst.

"Um, it's all clear, but you're gonna want to brace yourself."

"I can't brace myself," Gracie slurred. "I can barely stand up."

"Just hold onto me a little longer." I helped her walk through the door.

What was inside was *not* what I expected.

She was so out of it; she didn't even notice. I helped her to sit in the desk chair that Sunny had set in front of us. Her place had been ransacked as badly as her father's suite had been. Drawers were emptied, furniture overturned, items smashed. Couch cushions and the bed mattress had been slashed. Someone had been looking for something, but it felt different than her father's room.

This felt like pure evil.

I looked at Sunny for clarification.

"I can tell what you're thinking even without a mind reading ability, and you would be right. The negative energy is strong here. This is the handiwork of someone who is filled with hatred. And you haven't seen the worst of it yet." She gestured for me to follow.

In the bathroom, someone had written in red lipstick, *Pay for the sins of your father. It's your time.*

~

Sunny

"Slow down, Granny," I said into my cell the next morning from the Sky Deck. "I can barely hear you."

It had been a long night. The ship wasn't sold out, so the captain gave the go ahead for Gracie to move into a new room with a new medallion. She didn't have a clue what was going on, still out of it from the pain meds and getting attacked.

Eddie and Amy were going over her room with the CSI team, while Kalli and I took turns sitting by Gracie's new bedside, keeping watch to make sure she was okay. I'd slept in and had just gone up top to get some tea when my grandmother called.

"Granny, I said I can barely hear you," I repeated.

"Well, land sake's child, open your ears," Granny Gert replied. I could hear her moving about and just picture her buzzing around with her apron tied around her waist and her wooden spoon sticking out of the pocket. "Is this better?"

"Much," I replied with a smile, missing home. "Now, why did you call me? What happened again?"

"Do I need a reason to call my own granddaughter?"

I rubbed my temples, the beginning of a headache forming. "Of course not, but you said something happened."

"Oh, that's right." The sound of the oven door opening and the scrape of a cookie sheet sliding in filled her pause before she continued. "Well, now, Vivian was taking little Tina on a nature hike—"

I stopped walking, and a gust of wind pushed me back a step. "A hike? She's too little for that."

"The backyard of the inn, dear."

Relief shot through me. "Oh, well, that's fine, I guess."

Granny's laughter tinkled through the line. "You worry too much. Now let me finish my story before I forget. The mind's not what it used to be, you know."

"Oh please, your mind is as sharp as ever. Not much gets by you, Granny." I walked over to the railing and looked out over the rolling waves. "You were saying?"

"Well, I had just gotten back from giving my favorite swans, Fred and Ginger, some bread at Mini Central Park. They have brand new babies. Four of them. They're so cute, I just want to—"

I looked up at the dark clouds rolling across the sky. It was going to rain soon. "Granny, back to the hike." Her mind might be sharp, but Granny always had a lot to say and tended to get distracted.

"Oh, me, oh, my...right." More dishes clattered in her kitchen. "Anyway, when I got back to the inn, Vivian was showing Tina some flowers beneath the big ole oak tree out back when little River started to cry."

I gripped the railing as a big wave rocked the boat. "What's wrong with my baby? Is he okay?" Becoming a mother had made me realize how Mitch felt. Fiercely protective to keep my loved ones safe.

"Oh, he's right as rain. Talk about smart as a whip. That boy is special. Anyway, Donald was pushing him in the baby carriage, but River kept crying. When he started wailing, your mother took Tina's hand and walked back to your father to switch children because she said he wasn't *grandfathering* right." Granny's laughter tinkled through the line again. "*Grandfathering*. Why, whoever heard of such a thing."

"Granny, what happened? Is River okay?"

"Oh, fiddledeedee, that child is a prodigy. He has a gift like nothing I've ever seen before."

"What do you mean?"

"As soon as your mother and Tina walked away from the tree, that baby stopped crying. Calmed right down as happy as a clam. I've never understood that saying. How can someone tell if a clam is happy?"

"I don't know, Granny, but how does that make River special?"

"Well, because he saved their lives, of course. I'd call that pretty special."

"How on earth did a six-month-old baby save anyone's life?"

"A massive dead branch came crashing down from that big ole oak tree right where your mother and daughter had been standing just seconds before."

My stomach flipped. *He knew*. "What did they do?"

"That was it for the hike, and Vivian wanted that tree cut down, pronto. But that oak tree is older than Great Grandma Tootsie, and she's a century. So, your father calmed your mother down and then called the tree company to come give it a haircut. They trimmed away all the dead branches, and he looks good as new now. Problem solved. So, what's been happening on your end. Are you having a good time, dear?"

I laughed a little hysterically. "Lovely. I'm having a grand ole' time."

I'd survived the Devil's Triangle only to be stuck on a ship with a killer running around loose. Had to hide out in a morgue. Nearly drowned in a sinking lifeboat. Had to save my friend from being sawed in half. Learned how to push the tush. And babysat a poor beat up girl high on pain meds. I didn't think I could handle much more fun.

But I didn't want to worry my family any more than I had to. It sounded like they had their hands full just taking care of each other and my children. Or, rather, my children were taking care of them, apparently.

All the more reason to solve this murder and get home.

"That's nice, dear." A bell dinged. "Gotta go. My

cookies are done." My grandmother hung up, and I laughed so hard I cried.

Mitch walked over and handed me a cup of tea from Java Junction as the first fat raindrops began to fall.

"How are the kids?" he asked then frowned when I laughed harder.

I took a blessed sip wondering if it was too early to start drinking as I replied, "Right as rain."

16

KALLI

I sat at the round table in the captain's office on the bridge with Nik, Sunny, and Mitch. Amy and Eddie were there, as well as the captain. Tyrone was manning the bridge, and Justin was taking care of all other security matters.

"So where are we at?" Captain Hughes took off her hat and set it on the table in front of her.

"Chee Chee admitted she wears a golden blond wig, but claims she wasn't in Baron's room the day of his murder. She says that was the morning after the cyclone hit, and she was in Doctor Chopra's office, getting seasick meds." Mitch scanned his notes. "I checked with the doc, and she confirmed Chee Chee was there at the time the man overboard alarm sounded."

"What about last night when Gracie was attacked," the captain asked.

"She's back with Lance and said she was with him in his room at the time of the attack," Nik said.

"Lance confirmed the same thing." Agent Amy pulled a notebook out of her blazer and flipped through the pages. "He was also rehearsing his magic act at the time Baron was murdered. He rehearses alone in the privacy of his room so no one can see his tricks. His room is on the floor above Baron's on the same side of the ship. His room steward can verify he never left his room until after the man overboard alarm sounded."

"I spoke with Natalia at the spa," PI Eddie said with his hands clasped before him, no notebook in sight. "She admits she was jealous of how much time and attention Lance had been giving Gracie, but she would never hurt her. Ivan spoke up and said he was with Natalia the whole evening."

"Did Natalia confirm this?" the captain asked.

Eddie shrugged. "She didn't deny it."

"Gracie wouldn't tell us what she and Frankie talked about before she entered the ladies' room right outside of Knockin' Boots," I said, "but I find it odd that he never returned to work after that."

"We know he claims he was sick in his room, but he doesn't have anyone who can prove it," Sunny said. "I sensed evil in her room. Frankie strikes me as a lover not a fighter. I especially can't see him hurting a woman."

"Except, his wife is divorcing him. Rumor has it he was not only a cheater, but he was broke. He can't afford a divorce. Things are going to be messy," Nik said. "I'd say he might not love women so much at the moment."

"Good point," Mitch replied.

"All that Gracie's thoughts told me was that she felt guilty and that her father's death was all her fault." I strummed my fingertips on the table as I organized my thoughts. Realizing what I was doing, I quickly sanitized my hands. "What if Gracie was the one who killed her father? All she ever wanted was his attention, yet he kept her hidden away and wouldn't let her spend money because it might draw attention to her. He didn't want people asking questions. Greed and resentment are powerful motivators."

"So is love," Sunny said. "Gracie had no idea at the time how much her father truly did love her. He was protecting her from something...or someone." She nodded. "I think Gracie understands that now, and guilt is eating her up inside. The question is, what does she feel so guilty about?"

"What about Diana?" I asked.

The captain sat up straight, her back stiff as she cleared her throat. "What about Ms. North?" The captain knew that we knew they were a couple, but she didn't know that Mitch and Nik knew about it.

"Diana clearly didn't like Cara Carmichael. Diana didn't like that Baron was working closer with Cara than her in organizing the event," I clarified. "Maybe Diana murdered Baron out of anger. You have to consider all possibilities."

"Diana was discussing other events and whether or not we should still have them after the storm blew through. She was with me at the time of Baron's death." The captain folded her hands in front of her. "I can verify that."

"Okay, that's fair," I said.

"But what about Cara's disappearance?" Sunny looked around the room. "No one has an exact time that occurred, other than no one has seen her since her argument with Diana on the Sky Deck. Cara got your approval to have the auction for Abigail's art, even though the prized piece is still missing. From what I gather, Diana didn't like that. Now Cara is missing, and Diana is in charge. Seems to me, Diana got everything she wanted. Do you think Diana took Cara out to get her way?"

The captain sighed and pinched the bridge of her nose. "I don't know what to think anymore."

"What do you want us to do, Captain?" Eddie asked.

"Keep your eyes and ears open," she said gravely. "We can't hold these people at sea much longer."

"Aye aye, Captain." Eddie nodded.

"In the meantime, I'll have Officer Justin and his team search the ship top to bottom. Every floor, every room, every closet. If Cara is still alive like you say, Sunny, then we're not going to stop looking until we find her."

~

Sunny

"Where are you going?" Kalli asked, hurrying to catch up to me as we left the captain's office.

The guys had gone to the casino to see if they could find anything more about Milton and Mavis. I suspected they wouldn't mind playing a few rounds followed by a cigar, all in the name of work.

"I'm following a hunch." I headed for the elevators.

"What does that mean?"

"The room Cara was in was cold and dark. Almost like a storage room." I looked at her. "The only storage rooms I know of are on the lower floors for the crew."

"Hey, I'm your Sidekick Sister, remember?" Kalli kept pace beside me. "Where you go, I go."

"Then down we go." I made a beeline for the elevator that would take us to the crew floors like we took before.

"Didn't the captain say she was going to have the ship searched room by room?" Kalli looked at me as we stepped on the elevator and pressed the down button.

"Yes, but I don't trust they will get to her in time." I was already shaking my head, that feeling of doom escalating. "A human being can live thirty days without food but only three days without water. Time is of the essence I'm afraid."

"You sound like me." Kalli nodded. "Logic is something I understand." She eyed me curiously. "Where to?"

"I'm not really sure. I'm following my gut on this one." The elevator dinged on the bottom floor, and we stepped off. "I say we start at the bottom and work out way up since the security staff will start at the top and work their way down. Hopefully the answer will be somewhere in the middle."

"Did you have another vision?"

"No, but I'm going with my gut. It hasn't steered me wrong so far."

"Well, I hope you're right this time. I did some research before I came," Kalli said. "Below deck one, there is a tween deck zero and below that is the tank top floor negative one. These two decks are usually filled with machinery spaces. The turbines are huge. Then all the other non-essential components of a ship are there like the ballast, sewage, steering gear, various pumps, compressor, portable water tanks, etcetera."

"Which is why I skipped those. I saw a dark storage area. I don't think that's the right floor."

"Well, then there's deck one which is the deck where big refrigerators for food are stored, crew accommodations, along with the tween deck medical facility, jail, and morgue. We've already been there, and I for one don't care to go back." She shivered. "Then there's the *highway*, which is what crew members use to commute to work, deliver trolleys, and hang out. The galley, aka cafeteria, is on deck two aft."

"I have a feeling the highway floor is our answer. We'll steer clear of the morgue, I promise, but this crew passageway has plenty of storage facilities where she could be." I made my way down a long hallway. Crew members were coming and going in both directions. We didn't have uniforms of any kind on, so people kept giving us funny looks.

"I don't like being this low." Kalli's voice held her uneasiness. "There's no windows because we're below the water. That alone is terrifying. And if the power goes out again, we'll be plunged into darkness." She gripped Venus harder. "Good thing I have my purse. There's a flashlight in there." She picked up the pace to catch up to me. "Do you have any idea where we're going?"

I suddenly stopped, and she bounced off my back. "What is it?"

"I'm not sure," I said. "I just got a really strong feeling that we're close." I walked slowly, touching door after door, and then I froze. A cold numbness settled over me. "She's in here. I just know it."

"Cara? Are you in there?" Kalli asked.

Nothing.

Kalli tried the doorknob. "It's unlocked."

"Probably because it's just an old storage closet." I entered the room and looked for a light switch. Flicking the switch, nothing happened.

Kalli pulled out a flashlight from Venus. "Look, the lightbulb is out." She shined her flashlight around the room. Broken appliances, furniture, cabinets, and various other items filled the room.

"Maybe I was wrong," I said. "This looks like an

old junk storage closet. There's nothing of value in here."

"All the more reason that it would make a great hiding place. No one would have a reason to come in here until they reach port and can haul this stuff off to make room for items that get broken or damaged on the next cruise."

"But I don't see her anywhere, yet I have the strongest sensation that she's here. Or she was here at some point."

We searched the room and were just about to leave when I spotted the trunk.

"Oh, Lord, you don't think she's in there, do you?" Kalli held the light on the trunk and walked closer.

"It's locked," I said.

"What about this?" Kalli found a metal curtain rod in the corner and handed it to me. "This might work."

I took the piece of metal and threaded it through the ring the lock was on. Pulling it toward me, it wouldn't budge. "Here, grab on and let's pull together."

We braced our feet on the trunk and pulled as hard as we could. The ring cracked and the lock fell off. I tossed the metal rod aside and lifted the lid to the trunk.

There was Cara Carmichael curled into a ball.

"Is she dead?" Kalli squeaked.

I felt for a pulse and blew out a breath of relief. "No. She has a pulse, but it's faint. She looks so pale. I don't think she would have lasted another day."

"We need to get help." Kalli ran to the door and shouted for help.

Several crew members came running. Everyone talked at once, asking what happened and who Cara was and how she got in there. No one had answers, even us. Security was called and medical came. We waited for the stretcher, not wanting to move her in case her neck or spine were compromised.

Agent Amy and PI Eddie showed up at the same time as medical.

"How did you know where to look?" Eddie asked.

I shrugged. "Just a feeling I had. I followed my gut, and it led me here."

"Good work, ladies," Amy said.

"What's that?" Eddie asked as the medical team lifted Cara out of the chest.

Kalli sucked in a breath. "Is that what I think it is?"

Amy frowned. "What on earth is that doing in there?"

I stared down into the trunk at Abigail Hernandez's missing piece of art.

17

KALLI

"This has got to stop, Ma," I said into my cell phone from the Sky Deck.

After being so far beneath the water on Deck one, I needed air. I stood under a covered section of the upper deck, looking out over the dark sky and rolling waves. The rain came down in an intimidating torrential sheet now, but anything was better than the tomblike stuffy storage room. Cara was in the medical center, recovering. Thanks to Sunny's intuition, we'd found her just in time.

And thanks to Pop, the Coast Guard had *saved* Ma and Aunt Tasoula just in time.

"You no appreciate anything I do for you," Ma said.

"You could have died. All that's doing for me is making me worried," I said.

"We no die," Aunt Tasoula said. "We wear the wings."

"Wings?" I rubbed my throbbing temples.

"The water wings. You know, the thingy you blow up and put on you arms?" Aunt Tasoula clarified. "We no drown."

"Soula is crazy," Ma said. "I no wear wings." I

heard her pat her large bosom. "I wear the rubber duckie around my waist."

"'Tis true," Aunt Tasoula confirmed. "She got it stuck under the bosoms. I thought we would have to pop them to get her free. It can happen, you know. Poor cousin Penelope was never the same after her bosoms popped." I heard a rustle through the line and could just picture her making the sign of the cross.

"Soula, you nincompoop. My bosoms no go pop. Penelope's were those plant-based thingies. Mine are *real*. My Kalliope no take after me, but she no need the plants, either. I watered her well."

I couldn't even go there.

Shaking my head, I finally asked, "You think children's inflatables are going to save you two from getting run over in the harbor? This is the ocean we're talking about, and a huge port. Massive ships come in and out all the time. They would never see you."

"Oh, I pretty hard to miss." I could just picture my aunt patting her long, teased head of hair.

"What did you expect to do? Swim to me?"

"Don't be silly, Kalliope," Ma said. "We row, row, row the boat."

"It defective," Aunt Tasoula said. "We spin in circles like Isoce-round."

"*You* defective," Ma mumbled.

"You're both lucky the Coast Guard spotted you before something terrible happened." I sighed. "Can you both just please stay put until Nik and I get home?"

Ma and Aunt Tasoula started speaking at once, but I couldn't focus on what they were saying. Nik had appeared on the deck and was waving me over. I hurried to him with a questioning look on my face, still holding the phone to my ear.

"Cara Carmichael is awake," he said.

"A car?" Ma asked. "Who this Cara in a car with Michael?"

I blinked, remembering they were still on the line. "What?"

"That's it, Ophelia." I heard Aunt Tasoula snap her fingers. "We take the ferry."

I had no words...so I hung up.

"Was that the mamas?" he asked.

I just shook my head. "Wrong number."

Ten minutes later, Nik and I walked into the medical center to find Sunny and Mitch already there. Cara lay in a hospital bed with oxygen tubes coming out of her nose and an IV coming out of her arm. A machine with all sorts of readings beeped quietly beside her.

"She's awake," Sunny said.

"Thanks to you," I replied.

"Thank you both," Cara said weakly. She brushed away a tear. "I didn't think I was ever going to get out of that trunk. It felt like being buried alive."

"What happened?" I asked gently.

Mitch and Nik stood off to the side with their notebooks out.

"I really don't know." Cara looked off as if she were trying to remember. "I remember being thrilled that the captain had agreed to let Abigail's art auction go on as planned. That poor girl has been through enough with her prized piece of art gone missing and her whole private auction as an artist taking a backseat to a murder investigation. Rightfully, so, but I still feel bad for her. Diana wasn't happy that I got the go ahead. She insisted on taking over the event, but the captain sided with me."

I looked at Sunny and could tell she was thinking

the same thing. Diana had to be hurt and upset with the captain not backing her, especially given how close they were. "What happened next?"

"Well, I was going through Abigail's inventory and figuring out the best way to display the pieces, when one of the pedestals I was going to use broke. I took it down to the storage room for junk and spotted a quaint trunk. I was inspired to use it in her show." She shook her head. "I opened the lid to inspect it and was shocked to find Abigail's missing piece of art."

"I know how you felt," Sunny said. "We were shocked to discover it when the medical team pulled you out." Sunny's brow puckered. "How did you end up inside the trunk? It was locked on the outside, so I'm assuming you didn't put yourself in there."

Cara lifted her hands. "I honestly don't know. One minute I was standing there, and the next someone shoved me from behind. I never heard them coming and didn't see a thing. I hit my head on the lid and woke up inside the cold, dark, cramped space." She squeezed her eyes shut, and her voice hitched. "It felt like being in a coffin. I don't know how long I was in there, but I didn't think I was ever going to get out."

The beeps started getting louder on the machine.

Dr. Chopra adjusted something. "Okay, folks, why don't we let Ms. Carmichael rest now. I think she's been through enough, don't you?"

"Of course." Mitch handed Cara his card. "You're a strong woman, Ms. Carmichael. You'll get through this, and I can promise you, we won't stop looking until the person who did this to you is caught."

She nodded and wiped away more tears.

Nik handed his card to Cara as well. "If you think of anything else that might help, give us a shout. We've got you." He nodded firmly.

Sunny and I said our goodbyes, and the four of us left.

"What a day this has been," I said as we reached the atrium. "Where is the missing piece of art now?"

"Back with Abigail Hernandez, where it belongs," Sunny said. "The auction was a huge success. She sold out, all except for this last piece. I don't think she's going to let this one out of her sight."

"At least the mystery of the missing art is solved," I said.

"Found but not solved," Nik countered. "We still don't know who took it or why."

"And we still have a murder to solve." Mitch headed toward the elevator.

"Where are you going?" Sunny asked.

"Following *my* gut this time." Mitch punched the floor to the casino. "And I'm betting it's about to pay off."

~

Sunny

I had never been much of a gambler. I came from money but knew what it was like to have to work for every penny. When I first moved to Divinity, my parents had cut me off to try to force me to stay in the Big Apple. They'd both had such prestigious careers as a world-renowned cardiologist and highly respected lawyer.

They didn't know how to relate to their free-spirited psychic daughter.

Not to be deterred, I made my way as the local fortune-teller and later got paid to consult with the police. I was proud of all I had accomplished and liked knowing the outcome of things. Gambling was a game of chance I wasn't willing to roll the dice on. Milton Dubois, however, was clearly addicted.

Addicted people did desperate things.

Kalli and I followed Nik and Mitch through the casino. The interior was a vibrant, bustling space adorned with bright lights, colorful décor, and a constant hum of excitement. Rows of slot machines lined the floor, accompanied by the sound of jingling coins and occasional cheers.

We wove our way around table games like poker, blackjack, and roulette that were surrounded by players focused on their strategies. The air was filled with a mix of anticipation, chatter, and the occasional clinking of glasses from the bar.

The atmosphere was charged with energy and the thrill of chance.

Milton and Mavis sat at a Megabucks slot machine. He kept playing the game over and over. All at once, the reels came to a sudden stop, accompanied by a flurry of lights, sounds, and animations. The machine flashed with colorful graphics and played celebratory music, creating a sense of anticipation from the growing crowd.

The Megabucks slot machine landed on a set of numbers. A moment of intense excitement and disbelief registered across Milton's face. Realization sunk in that the winning combination had been hit. Milton shouted with a rush of adrenaline and joy while Mavis's face registered pure relief. Cheers rang out from hopeful onlookers, hovering nearby for a chance at the machine.

It was a thrilling and surreal experience to behold. I'd never seen anyone win big before. We made our way through the crowd and stared at the game.

Milton had won the jackpot of over several million dollars.

Guess *new* money wasn't so bad after all.

The casino staff escorted Milton to cash out. Mitch and Nik followed close behind, with Kalli and me bringing up the rear. A flurry of people swarmed into his seat at the slot machine, while others walked along with him, asking what his secret was.

How did he choose the winning machine?

Was there a certain time of day that was luckier?

How much did he pay into the machine before winning?

Milton was glowing with excitement and loving every minute of it. Meanwhile, Mitch and Nik had their hands full, helping the casino's security team to keep the mob from trampling the old man. Kalli and I slowed our pace to give Mavis a little extra space. We didn't need her collapsing again.

"How are you doing, Mavis?" I asked.

"Better now." Her voice reflected her relief.

"That's so exciting that Milton won so much money," Kalli said.

"It certainly is," she said, adding half under her breath, "we could sure use it."

"But I thought you were from old money," I said.

Mavis looked startled over revealing so much out loud. She cleared her throat. "Oh, well, I mean you can't live forever on old money, you know."

"Speaking of living and one's health," Kalli added, looking concerned, "have you set up any doctor appointments for when you get back home?"

"Oh, no." Mavis shook her head and held up her hands. "Who knows when that will be. I'm feeling much better, dear. I'll be okay. Don't you go worrying about me."

Milton came back with Mitch and Nik beside him. "We're all set, lovie. I had them do a bank transfer."

"What are you going to spend all that money on?" I asked.

"How about paying the cruise line back for starters," Nik said.

We all looked at him, startled.

Milton's face paled, but he didn't say anything.

"I knew we were hurting, but what did you do, Milton?" Mavis sounded fragile and looked old all of a sudden.

"I'm so sorry, lovie. I didn't mean to. I just couldn't help myself." He held up his checkbook. "But you see, it was all worth it. We won."

"This time we won. What about all the other times we lost? Wasn't pawning my great grandmother's brooch enough?" She looked hurt and disappointed in him.

"I'll get help this time; I promise."

"I sure hope that you do, Milton," Mitch said. "In the meantime, you're under arrest for insurance fraud."

This time Milton was the one who dropped to the floor, out cold.

18

KALLI

Milton and Mavis sat in the captain's office on the bridge. After he passed out, he was thoroughly examined by Dr. Chopra. Everyone agreed he didn't pose a threat to anyone. And he certainly wasn't going anywhere, out in the middle of the ocean.

So, he was released on his own recognizance.

Mavis was beside herself, worrying about him and horrified over what he had done. The doctor was most concerned about her having another episode and ordered her to rest. She, of course, refused. Wherever her Milton went, she went, too.

"Mr. Dubois, are you going on the record and officially stating that your wife didn't know about your insurance fraud scheme to gain money to feed your gambling addiction?" Captain Hughes asked with a pen poised over a piece of paper.

She sat at the head table with PI Eddie, Agent Amy, Officer Justin, Mitch, Nik, Sunny, and me. The silence in the room was deafening.

"She's been on a lot of trips with you, all expenses paid," the captain continued. "Did she ever once ask you where the money came from?"

Mavis sat next to her husband, sniffling. "*She* is right here. I was the one who was born into money. Why on earth would I ask where the money came from to go on a trip when that's the lifestyle I have led since I was born?" Mavis looked at her husband. "Tell her, Milton. Answer the captain."

"It's true. My lovie has always been wealthy, but that's not why I married her. She is the love of my life." He looked so full of remorse, regret, and shame. "I didn't always have a gambling addiction. For a long time, I was in denial. It was lovie who opened my eyes to the truth. She tried to get me to stop, but I can be stubborn. Anyone else might have left me, but not once did my lovie turn her back on me. Not even when I blew through her inheritance and then pawned her heirloom brooch." His voice hitched. "I don't deserve her."

Mavis sighed. "For better or worse is what we vowed. I don't take that lightly." She reached out and took his hand in her own. "I'll always be here for you, no matter what. But I can't help you if you're in jail."

The captain nodded and made a few notes.

"Where did the insurance fraud come into play?" Mitch asked.

"Five years ago, we were on a cruise with friends from our social circle. The money from lovie's brooch was running out. I knew we were on borrowed time if we wanted to keep living the lifestyle she'd always known. I couldn't take that away from her, too. When a member of our group got food poisoning and died, the cruise line paid his family handsomely."

"Our sources say that you didn't like that man any more than you liked Baron Von Wielig," Nik said, narrowing his eyes.

"Did you kill that man back then, looking for money?" Mitch asked, "and then kill Baron this time, looking for his?"

"Good heavens, no," Milton sputtered. "I'm not always the easiest to get along with, but I'm not a murderer."

"How does the insurance fraud come into play?" The captain stared him down.

"I saw an opportunity. I faked an injury, and the insurance paid rather than have me sue." He looked sheepish.

"Milton Michael Dubois," Mavis said. "What about the other injuries? I just thought you were accident prone. You should be ashamed of yourself."

"It's what has kept us going for the past five years." He bowed his head. "I am so ashamed. I knew it was wrong. I just couldn't stop." He lifted tear-filled eyes. "Addiction is a terrible thing."

A heavy pause filled the room.

"Are you sure Mavis wasn't in on it?" Eddie looked from Milton to Mavis, watching them closely, his square jaw all hard intimidating angles. "Did you fake your heart ailment aboard this cruise? Was that part of the masterplan?"

"I should say not." She sat up straighter, looking stronger than she had earlier. "I would never stoop so low."

"I believe her," Amy said, squinting at her. "I can read people very well. It's one of the things I'm known for. Besides, Dr. Chopra diagnosed her."

"I believe her, too," Sunny added, looking at Milton. "I believe them both, actually. I've seen their past. They are good people. Milton just lost his way for a bit. There has to be something that can be worked out. I don't think either of them will survive Milton going to jail. It won't be good for anyone, including the cruise line."

"What do you want to do, Captain?" I asked. The captain of a ship was the highest command when at sea.

The captain stared at them both for a long moment before giving her decision.

"Well, I can talk to my superiors. I think if Milton takes his earnings from the casino on this ship and pays back all the fraudulent money he spent over the past five years, then they won't make him go to jail. I think everyone will be better served if he got help for his addiction and did so many hours of community service for the cruise line." She looked at Milton. "What do you think, Mr. Dubois? Does that sound like a fair deal to you?"

"More than fair." His eyes filled with tears. "And that will leave just enough money to start over and pay for the procedure Mavis needs. That's all I really care about. Spending the remainder of my years with my lovie."

"Now, there's the man I married." Mavis patted his hand.

"In the meantime, you're banned from the casino." The captain pointed a finger at him. "I mean it. Don't test me."

Milton nodded. "I wouldn't dream of it."

~

Sunny

Later that evening, the weather had cleared, and a pleasant breeze wafted across the ocean. A far cry from the stormy weather earlier. Kalli and I had come up top to the Sky Deck to get some fresh air and take a break. Dallas and Simon entertained people by the pool while we watched.

Mitch and Nik were working with the captain and their sources to close the deal for Milton. Amy was questioning Cara further to see if she could think of anything at all to link someone to the art theft and see if it had anything to do with Baron's murder. While Eddie was questioning Gracie further to see if she could help pinpoint her attacker and narrow down any possible motives for Baron's murder. Meanwhile, we told the captain about the nanny cam, and she had Justin working with his security team, still searching the rest of the floors for the nanny cam.

"Hey, look, there's Gracie." Kalli pointed over by the bar.

Gracie spotted us and headed over to our table.

"Have a seat and join us." I pointed to the chair next to me. "How are you feeling? You look stronger, and your color is better."

"I'm feeling a little more like myself. I never got to thank you both for staying with me. Eddie showed me the pictures of what happened to my old room. I'm still in shock and a little spooked over that message on the mirror." She crossed her arms over her middle and sat down. "Who would want to hurt me?"

A gust of wind swept over the deck, bringing the smell of sea spray with it.

Kalli grabbed her wine glass before it could blow over. "Someone who wanted to get at your father, I think. It's the only thing that makes sense."

"He did have a lot of enemies," Gracie admitted then looked at us. "My mother died giving birth to me. I really relate to Abigail Hernandez. We have the same background, and she lost her mother as well. Her art speaks to me."

"She's very talented," Kalli said. "I bought a piece of her work for my new house with Nik. I can't wait to show it to him. It's going to be a surprise."

"That's sweet," Gracie replied.

"So, tell us more about your relationship with your father." I looked at her.

Gracie shrugged. "My grandmother raised me. I didn't meet my father until years later. I thought he was embarrassed of me, and that's why he kept me hidden." She shook her head, tears starting to well in her eyes.

"What's wrong?" I gave her hand a squeeze.

"I didn't believe him when he told me to be careful. That if people knew he had a child, they would use me to get to him. I only flirted with the men on this ship to make my father angry, but he was right. I was playing a foolish game. The men didn't like me for me. They only wanted my father's money." A sob slipped out. "I can't take the guilt anymore. It's all my fault that he's dead."

"What makes you think that?" Kalli asked.

"Because I—"

A loud argument broke out over at the bar.

We all looked at each other and ran over to see what the fuss was about.

"Why did you do it?" Frankie was shouting at Courtney, looking like he'd completely come unhinged. His hair was a mess, his clothes wrinkled, and he had a crazed look in his eyes. Gone was the charming young man we'd met on night one.

Courtney lifted her shoulder and set a few drinks on a tray, looking like she didn't have a care in the world. "I don't know what you're talking about."

That seemed to infuriate him.

"Yes, you do! She told me." He took a step toward her from behind the bar. "My marriage has been over for a while now, but I'm broke. I was trying to make enough money to divorce her first. Why would you tell my wife about what I do on this ship? It's none of your business."

"Because you're a cheater, just like my ex-husband!" Courtney shouted back. "I hate cheaters, and she deserves to know."

"I'm going to be ruined because of you," he growled.

"Good." She snapped her gum. "Frankly, my dear, I don't give a—"

"You will when I'm through with you!" He lunged at her and wrapped his latex gloved hands around her neck.

Everything happened at once.

People started scrambling out of the way. Glasses flew off the bar, bottles smashed, trays and garnishes went flying. Spectators screamed. Total chaos ensued. Chief Officer Justin and his team appeared from out of nowhere.

Officer Roger grabbed Courtney.

Chief Justin secured Frankie.

"Frankie, what are you doing?" Gracie shook all over, her face putting the puzzle pieces together. "You're the one who attacked me, aren't you?"

Frankie stopped moving and his face paled. "No, I was in bed sick."

Gracie's face filled with disgust. "Yeah, *after* you threatened me to keep quiet about the watch."

"What watch?" I asked.

"The watch you found in the lifeboat," Gracie snarled, her eyes not leaving Frankie. "I gave it to

Frankie because he needed money. He said he wanted to divorce his wife once he was out of debt. That he wanted to be with me when it was all over. I know now that was all lies."

"What happened," Kalli asked.

"He tried to pawn it in Bermuda, but it wasn't worth anything. I was as shocked as he was that it was a fake. Then he panicked, so I gave him the room key, and he tried to put it back into my father's safe." Her eyes widened in horror as she whispered, "You killed my father, too, didn't you?"

Frankie shook his head violently. "No, I swear. He caught me in his room returning the watch. He wouldn't listen to me. We struggled and he fell, so I ran. But he was very much alive when I left him."

"You work on this ship," I said, working things out in my brain. "You know where the security cameras are and how to avoid them. You would have made sure to enter his room at a time when you knew he wasn't there. So *how* did Baron catch you?"

"With this." Justin held up the nanny cam.

Everyone gasped.

That was the exact nanny cam I saw in my vision.

"I'm pretty sure this will give us the answers we're looking for," Justin said.

"You were so desperate after finding out my father's watch was a fake, so you stole the art and hid it where you thought no one would look. You planned to smuggle it off the ship when we dock in New York City, didn't you?" Gracie paced back and forth.

"No, you have it all wrong," Frankie pleaded.

"What I don't get, is why attack me?" Gracie went on, not really listening to him. "Was it out of anger for everything going wrong in your own life? It wasn't my fault his watch was a fake. You knew I didn't have any money of my own."

"You do now as Baron's sole heir," I said gently. "He loved you more than you know and left you everything. I saw his will in a vision."

Gracie blinked at me. "You did?"

I nodded.

"You don't need a man to take care of you, Gracie." Kalli squeezed her hand. "You're going to be able to take very good care of yourself." She smiled. "We're thankful for you as well." She winked.

"You have to believe me. I'm telling the truth. I didn't kill anyone," Frankie pleaded, kicking and screaming as security took him away.

Courtney clapped every step of the way.

It was over. I inhaled the deepest breath I'd taken since we started this cruise and pictured my darling little bundles of joy.

Maybe now we could finally go home.

19

KALLI

"**I** want to thank you all for your help," Captain Hughes said the next morning in her office at our round table meeting.

It had been a long night of tying up loose ends, but it was finally over. We were going home. I felt giddy with relief at the thought of my feet hitting dry land. I sipped my hot tea without a straw. Progress. The captain had called us all to a meeting and ordered a special bon voyage breakfast as the ship was being readied.

We were setting sail in an hour.

"We never would have solved Baron Von Wielig's murder without you all."

"Or found the missing art," Agent Amy said.e

"Not to mention solved the attempted murder of Cara Carmichael," PI Eddie interjected.

"That's all true." The captain nodded. "I've always been one to go with my gut. It's never led me astray. You ladies are pretty special." Diana still hadn't forgiven her siding with Cara, but I had a feeling the captain would be just fine. She was a strong, competent woman and a great captain.

"Thank you, Captain," Sunny said. "It was a pleasure consulting with you."

"Yes, I was happy to help," I added. "Consulting officially on a murder investigation was a first for me. I informally help Detective Stevens back home, but it was satisfying knowing I made a difference on this cruise." She looked at me with appreciation, and for a moment, I thought maybe she had read *my* mind.

Her gaze turned to Nik and Mitch, and she tipped her hat to them. "Gentlemen, I can admit when I'm wrong. You're both great detectives, and your assistance was invaluable. I'm glad I listened to your lovely ladies. They're pretty remarkable."

"They sure are." Mitch looked at Sunny with adoration, then he nodded once at the captain. "We were happy to help."

"It was our pleasure, Captain." Nik tilted his head at the captain, and then his gaze slid to me. "We won the jackpot with these two." His brilliant blue eyes sparkled with love and affection. This man had my whole heart.

The rest of the meal was eaten in silent reflection and gratitude. I didn't think I would ever cruise again, but I did have to admit I had grown a lot. Overcome a few fears and learned to cope with a few others. If we could survive the Bermuda Triangle and stay alive through a murder investigation, then I was pretty sure living together couldn't possibly be as hard as I was imagining. His St. Bernard, Woolfgang, and my calico cat, Prissy, would just have to learn to get along.

How hard could it be?

After our breakfast debrief, we all headed out of the office and onto the bridge to say our goodbyes and go pack. Suddenly, Officer Justin whipped the door open and stormed onto the bridge out of breath.

"Officer Cho, what's wrong?" Captain Hughes asked.

"There's a disturbance out on the Sky Deck," he said. "A passenger is insisting on speaking with you. He seems confused, disoriented, and a little in shock. "Come with me. This is something you have to see for yourself."

What could possibly be happening now? We all looked at Sunny. She held up her hands at a loss. We didn't waste any more time following Justin out of the bridge and onto the Sky Deck, then stopped short.

Rafe Overton stood before us, looking a whole lot less confident and debonaire. He was wearing the same clothes he'd had on when Sunny and I first met him in the little shop in Bermuda. Except he was a disheveled wreck. His clothes were dirty. His hair was a tangled mess. He had soot on his face.

I covered my nose. He smelled terrible.

"What's your name, son?" Captain Hughes asked.

"Oh, thank God, someone believes I belong on this ship," he said with a shaky voice. "My name is Rafe Overton."

The captain was nodding. "I've seen you on board with our own celebrity, Angela Rose, though never looking quite like this."

"Who?" Rafe scratched his head. "I don't know an Angela, and I haven't seen you since day one. Your crew picked me up on a dingy and accused me of jumping ship. Ask him." He thrust his hand at Justin.

"It's true. He didn't have his medallion on him, but I recognized his face. When we brought him on board to question him, he wasn't making any sense."

"I was making perfect sense, but you wouldn't listen." Rafe was clearly getting agitated. I recognized the signs of his anxiety spiraling. "I had to escape them to get to you." He was still breathing hard.

The captain raised her brows, looking around at us for input, but we were just as confused. She looked back at him. "Calm down, Mr. Overton. I'm listening now. Who are the people you're talking about? What happened?"

"A nightmare, that's what happened. I missed the entire cruise. One minute I was in Bermuda buying water shoes, trying to work up the nerve to do an excursion. Then I thought, who am I kidding. Stick with your comfort zone, Rafe. So I headed to an art gallery."

Sunny looked at me with eyes that said, *I knew he was into art!*

"I had just made my purchase and left the art gallery," Rafe continued, "when a bald man about my size and age approached me. I hadn't seen him on the ship, so I figured he lived on the island. He started asking me a bunch of questions. He kept trying to get me to go with him on an adventure, but my mama didn't raise no fool. I firmly told him no, even though I was shaking in my water shoes."

"Okay, so what happened then?" The captain looked confused. "I have to agree with Officer Cho. You're not making much sense."

Rafe threw up his hands in frustration. "I was *taken*, okay? Just like in the movie. They kept me in some cold, dark, nasty warehouse. Except, they didn't tell me why. I thought I was going to die on that island. I might not be brave, but I am smart. I know about old buildings. I'm an architect back home and design art galleries. So when I calmed down and realized they'd tied me to a wooden beam, I found the weak spot and pulled hard enough so it gave way. I didn't trust anyone on the island, so I ran straight to the harbor. They had taken my wallet and my medallion, so I didn't have a way to rent something. When I saw a small, motorized fishing boat, I stole it and didn't look back until I reached the ship."

"That's quite a story, Mr. Overton. The problem is we've seen you with Angela Rose all week."

"I'm telling you; I don't know anyone by the name of Angela Rose." He started to pace. "This is crazy. I feel like I'm on an episode of the Twilight Zone and..." his eyes grew huge and mouth fell open.

"Rafe, are you okay? You look like you've seen a ghost." I touched his arm. *It can't be...am I a twin?*

We all turned in the direction he was looking and stared in disbelief.

The confident debonair Rafe that we had gotten to know all week just walked onto the Sky Deck with Gracie Marks in deep conversation.

~

Sunny

As Granny Gert would say, *Well, fiddledeedee and bless my stars...What in the world is going on, child?*

Two Rafe Overtons?

All commotion and talking ceased until the Sky Deck was deathly quiet.

Gracie and Smooth Operator Rafe stopped walking and talking as if they just now realized something was going on. They looked around and both saw Hot Mess Rafe at the same time.

Gracie's smile slipped.

Smooth Operator Rafe's face hardened.

Hot Mess Rafe's eyes bulged.

"That's him!" Hot Mess Rafe thrust his finger in Smooth Operator Rafe's direction. "That's the man who lured me away. I would know those eyes anywhere."

Smooth Operator Rafe grabbed Gracie and yanked her in front of him, pulling out a plastic gun made from a 3D printer from inside his coat jacket.

Gracie gasped.

A muscle in Mitch's jaw bulged, and Nik clenched his hands into fists.

They had to be so frustrated because they weren't allowed to bring weapons on board. That wasn't the case with Eddie. He pulled his concealed carry from beneath his untucked shirt and out of the waistband of his jeans. A 9mm from the looks of it.

Being married to Mitch had taught me a thing or two about guns.

"Don't do anything stupid," Imposter Rafe snarled, looking like a totally different person. "This gun might be plastic, but it shoots very real bullets and passes a metal detector every time."

"What's going on?" Angela Rose appeared, her confused gaze reaching everyone in the room.

"Who are you?" Gracie sputtered while breaking free of the imposter's grasp.

He pulled off his gold and white wig, revealing a gleaming bald head. Then he peeled off his fake mustache, looking at Mitch and Nik.

Nik whistled long and slow.

Mitch narrowed his eyes and shook his head.

"You want to tell them, or should I, detectives?" Imposter Rafe smirked at the men.

"Marco DeLuca aka The Silent Hammer," Mitch said. "I haven't seen you since I left the city."

"I've heard of him." Nik rubbed his heavily

whiskered jaw. "Works for a notorious loan shark named Raven Bloodworth, who wasn't afraid to have DeLuca lay the hammer down to get her money back, with interest."

"That's right," Mitch said, adding, "DeLuca is a master of disguise." The scar on Mitch's jaw pulsed. "And even more deadly."

"Rafe...or Marco...or whoever you are, what have you been doing? I thought we were friends. I thought we had something special." Angela looked at him with eyes full of hurt and disillusion.

Marco's face softened for a moment. "It's been fun, doll face, but it could never last between us. You would eventually have found out who I was, and then I would have had to kill you. Such a shame."

Angela gasped and stepped back, bumping into Elton.

"You're a monster." Elton placed himself between Angela and the imposter, pointing a finger at the other man's chest. She seemed to visibly relax over his show of support instead of working against her.

"You have no idea, Music Man." Marco tipped his head at the detectives. "Thanks for the shoutout, boys." Then his smirk faded as he looked at Eddy with cold, hard eyes. "Drop the gun, Eddie, or I'll work the princess over again right before your eyes."

"You're the one who attacked me?" Gracie squeaked. "Why?"

You did those horrible things to her?" Angela's voice carried on a whisper as if the blinders had been removed and she was seeing Marco's true colors for the first time.

Marco shrugged, not bothered in the least by Angela's emotional state, then turned back to Gracie. "I told you that you had to pay for the sins of your father." Marco paused to glare into Gracie's frightened eyes. "Your daddy owed my boss a lot of money and tried to run from his obligation by hiding out on a cruise." He laughed harshly. "Stupid fool. No one can hide from the hammer."

"But my father had plenty of money."

I shook my head and stepped toward Gracie. "Your father had your inheritance secured in a safe account under an alias, waiting for you. He made some bad investments, but he would never use your money to pay back what he owed. I suspect he sold his real watches and replaced them with fakes to finance his lifestyle. I told you he really did love you. He wasn't about to let anyone take what was yours."

"Huh, I didn't think you were the real deal." Marco grunted. "Maybe I should have taken you instead."

A growl came from deep within Mitch's throat, and he was poised to pounce. One touch of my hand on his shoulder, and he stilled instantly. That didn't mean he wasn't tense and ready to strike at a moment's notice. Surely Marco was smart enough to sense that.

"Between my husband and my immortal cat, you wouldn't stand a chance," I said, hiding my fear and giving him a heads up in case he wasn't that smart. One thing was certain. The man was pure evil.

He was the negative energy I had felt all along.

Marco laughed harshly. "That might be an interesting challenge to take on, but I'm pressed for time." He looked to the sky. "My ride should be here soon." He yanked Gracie back against his chest and tightened his arm around her neck. "I want what Daddy Dearest owes my boss...and I'm thinking a little extra for me since he made me go to such trouble."

"I told you; I don't know where anything is. I have

to wait until I get home and his lawyer contacts me." Gracie's voice hitched. "Why did you have to kill him?"

"I didn't. Not saying I wouldn't have, but I hadn't made my move yet when the storm struck. If you saw the nanny cam, You would know Frankie is the one who got caught red handed with the watch in in your father's room. He admitted they fought. Frankly, I didn't think he had it in him to commit murder, but hey, he made my job easier. I was about to make my move the next day, but Daddy Dearest was already dead. So, I trashed your room to see what you had."

"You stole my trunk with the art in it, didn't you?" Gracie's voice hitched.

"Honey, that would have only taken a dent out of what your father owed." Marco scoffed. "And for the record," he said loudly in the direction of Eddie, Amy, Mitch and Nik. "There was no trunk in your room when I was in there. I would have taken a piece of art, but there's no way I could make a trunk disappear."

Kalli gasped, her gaze locking in mine.

I sucked in a sharp breath, and we shared a look of recognition with each other as another piece of this kaleidoscope of clues fell into place.

And Gracie Marks fainted, dead away.

Eddie, Mitch, and Nik all lunged at a surprised Marco who made the mistake of looking down for a split second at the motionless Gracie at his feet. He whipped his eyes back up and raised his gun, but Eddie got off a shot first.

He was an expert marksman.

The gun flew out of Marco's hand before he could squeeze the trigger. He grabbed his empty, burned palm in outrage and agony.

Mitch tackled him hard, his face within inches of Marco's. "Don't ever threaten my wife again."

Eddie tossed his handcuffs to Nik, who cuffed Marco's hands behind his back once Mitch flipped him over. "What, is your hammer a rubber mallet?" Nik snorted. "You're not so tough now, are you pal?"

"That's my man." Kalli sighed dreamily.

I grabbed her arm until she looked at me as I thought for her ears only....

This isn't over yet. We've got work to do.

20

KALLI

Once Marco DeLuca had been secured in the brig with Frankie, Eddie made a call to his contacts and had the helicopter carrying Raven Bloodworth intercepted. They had enough evidence and her right-hand man, who was singing like a canary, not willing to take the fall alone for her.

Gracie Marks Von Wielig would be just fine.

Cruise director Diana was a professional. She might not like that the captain had sided with Cara over her, but the captain stood tall and firm. Her personal life was separate from her professional one, and she would always do the right thing and put her ship first.

Putting her differences aside, Diana remained professional as well, and did her job. She handed the microphone to Captain Hughes and stepped back from the platform right outside the bridge. The captain nodded her thanks.

"This is your captain speaking," Captain Hughes said, her voice coming over the microphone and the loudspeaker throughout the ship. "This has certainly been a cruise for the record books, folks. I appreciate everyone's cooperation in staying calm during this investigation. I'm happy to say everyone is safe. The case is closed, and the lockdown is over. Let's go home."

Everyone cheered, and the captain handed the microphone back to Diana. People were buzzing with conversation as the captain went back on the bridge.

"We don't have much time before we reach port. What are we going to do?" I asked Sunny as we still stood on the Sky Deck, watching the water as the ship pulled anchor and began to move.

"I *knew* you were thinking the same thing as me when you heard what Marco said!" Sunny put her hands on her hips.

"Yes." I nodded, looking around to be sure we were out of earshot.

Mitch and Nik were helping Eddie and Justin with Marco and Frankie in the brig down below. Mavis and Milton hadn't left their room, putting themselves in house arrest once they heard everything else that was happening. Mavis didn't want any more trouble, and stated her traveling days were over. Meanwhile, Amy was wrapping up her paperwork with the captain on the bridge as the rest of the crew set sail.

All that was left of our investigative team was Sunny and me.

"What are we going to do about this?" Sunny asked.

"Well, we have to be careful," I replied, forming a plan in my mind. "We can't just go around throwing accusations without proof." I looked at my partner in crime. "But we *can* do what we do best and give the people a show for the ride home. I've always heard that truth is stranger than fiction."

"And always comes out." Sunny clapped her hands. "Are you thinking what I'm thinking?"

"Mystical Mavens here we come." I winked.

"Wow, you really have come along way, baby, as they say." Sunny laughed.

"Anything to get home." I laughed. "Follow me. I have an idea."

We crossed the Sky Deck to the stage where Dallas and Simon stood. I even let Dallas hook me with his imaginary fishing pole and reel me up the stairs, no matter how ridiculous I felt. I briefly wondered if imaginary fishing line was sanitary when Dallas waited a beat. *Oh, no you don't, mister.* I gave him a look that said, *squirming around like a fish on the end of the line is a hard no.*

Sunny took her imaginary net, clipped the line, and scooped me up with a wink. I chuckled, happy to follow *her* anywhere. Dallas clapped, thrilled that we played along in our own way. Good. It would make him more amenable to my idea.

Simon was asking him about ideas to keep the guests entertained until we reached port. Perfect timing. I told them about my idea, and they were thrilled. Simon helped us set up the stage, while Dallas took the microphone and spoke.

"Guess what, folks. I have a special treat for you all. The Mystical Mavens are back right here on our stage. So for all you people who've been dying to have a reading done, now's your chance."

Sunny and I spent the next couple of hours reading people, with Brie and Haden Gray capturing every moment on film and video. People were loving it. Past lives, present day, and future. Boy oh boy did I hear more thoughts than I cared to. Knowing too much about your fellow passengers wasn't always a good thing.

"Now *there's* a man with special talents." Sunny pointed to a man who had just walked onto the Sky

Deck. "Let's give a round of applause for our favorite Magic Man." Everyone clapped, and he stopped short, giving us a wary smile. "Come on up here, Lance. Give your audience a treat and let us predict your future."

He started waving his arms in front of him. "Oh, no, I don't think—"

The audience drowned out his words by chanting his name over and over. They refused to let him leave the Sky Deck until he played along. So, he held up his hands and nodded, making his way through the crowd to the stage.

"Have a seat, Magic Man." I pointed to the table like the one we had used during our show in Poseidon's Palace Theater.

He sat down, and the crowd grew quiet, fascinated. "Now what?" He played along, but it was clear by his eyes that he didn't believe in our gifts.

"Each of us will hold one of your hands, so we form a triangle." Sunny watched him closely.

"The Bermuda Triangle?" He chuckled, taking our hands. "You guys are good."

"You're about to find out just how good we really are," I said. "Think you can handle it?"

"Oh, I think I'll be fine." *This ought to be good.*

"I think *you'll* be good." I smiled.

His smile slipped a smidgen.

Sunny closed her eyes and started to breathe deeply. "Relax, Mr. Beckman. Don't be nervous."

"I'm not nervous. I can saw you in half, remember?"

"Or make us disappear," I said.

He frowned then cleared his throat. "Right."

"I see you've been busy this past year," Sunny stated. "You've worked for a lot of different ships for this cruise line."

"So do a lot of the crew." He shrugged. "That's common knowledge." *See, I knew they were fakes.*

Sunny opened her eyes. "How long have you been sick?"

His face turned deathly pale. "You're mistaken." *How did she know? That's not public knowledge. With HIPPA laws, there's no way she could have known, unless....*

"Oh, we're not mistaken, Lance," I said. "We're the real thing, and we know a lot more than just your health history."

"I saw it all, Lance," Sunny said. "There's no sense in denying anything. If you cooperate and tell the truth, things will go easier for you."

Lance jerked his hands away from ours and stood. "You don't know what you're talking about."

The crowd had grown bigger, and the captain and Amy had come off the bridge to see what was happening. Lance looked at them a little wildly, and then back at us. He was surrounded. There was nowhere to run or hide.

"I'm afraid we do," I said. "Like Rafe, or rather, Marco said, there was no way he could make that trunk disappear. Sunny came to the same conclusion I did, and I knew if she read you, she would see the truth."

"That's right, and I did," Sunny said. "Baron hid the art in Gracie's room in her trunk, knowing if no one suspected she was his daughter, then they would never look there. You got poor, gullible Gracie to tell you about her secret. She was distraught over giving Frankie the watch that was a fake and slipped up when she said she should have given him the sculpture instead."

"You knew where Baron hid the art," I said. "You knew Gracie had a thing for Frankie, we all did."

"That's right," Sunny said. "So when she spent the night with him during the storm, you went to her room and found the trunk."

"You're both crazy. Chee Chee will verify I was with her all night long. She's my alibi. Tell them, Chee Chee."

Chee Chee nodded. "It's true."

"You're right," Sunny said. "It *is* true. Chee Chee spent the night with you, and you drugged her. That was why the next morning she had to go to the doctors. She wasn't seasick from the storm."

Chee Chee gasped. "Why, you no good lying weasel. I should have known better. You let Natalia think you were a thing only to cheat on her with me. Then you got close to Cara probably to find out what she knew from Baron. You told me you were only helping her with the auction now that Baron was gone, and Diana was being crazy. You said poor Gracie was so young and on her own, so you were like a big brother to her. You used me to be your alibi."

"I didn't do anything." Lance glared at Sunny and me. "You can't prove anything. Ask the room steward. I never left my room until after the man overboard alarm went off. He'll verify my alibi."

"You would have gotten away with it if you hadn't been so greedy," Sunny said. "You turned on some music loud enough for the room steward to hear so he would know you were still in there, but you were a gymnast back in high school."

"Again, that's public record." He started to sweat. "You're trying to frame me."

"We're in the middle of the ocean, and Sunny just read you," I said. "When would we have had time to look into public records?" I shook my head. "You're doing a good job of framing yourself, Magic Man."

Sunny continued, "Your gymnast abilities made it easy for you to climb out onto your balcony and down to Baron's. How convenient that your room is directly above his."

"Because this plan was pre-meditated," I said.

"It certainly looks that way. You had just reached Baron's balcony when you saw Frankie run out of Baron's room with the nanny cam. Frankie knew where the cameras were, but he hadn't counted on Baron being paranoid and setting up one of his own. Baron got an alert, so he went back to catch Frankie in the act of returning the watch. They struggled, and then Frankie ran off with the teddy bear."

"Exactly. He killed him, not me," Lance said, then paled.

"So you admit you were there," I said.

"I admit nothing," he said.

"You don't have to," Sunny continued. "You entered the room, thinking Baron was already dead, so you put on gloves and trashed his place, looking for anything else of value. You never expected Baron to wake up. When he saw you, he ran, so you followed him. You were desperate to keep up your ruse, so when he climbed up to the lifeboat, you choked him and then threw him overboard, but you left the watch, hoping to frame Frankie."

"What about Marco?" Lance said. "He wore a wig with gold hair. That could be the hair in Baron's room and his watch."

"How did you know that information? It was private to the case." I studied him.

He remained silent.

"It doesn't matter. The hair from Marco's wig is not

the hair that was found at the crime scene," Sunny said. "You had Chee Chee's gold hair still on your clothes when you went to Baron's room and moved the watch."

"Like Marco said, when he went to Baron's room, he was gone and his room was already trashed, so he got friendly with Gracie and later trashed her room and beat her up when he wasn't finding anything of value," I said, pointing at Lance. "He's a killer, all right, but he's not our cruise ship killer. *You* are! You not only committed art theft, but you also committed murder and attempted murder."

"That right," Sunny said. "Later, when you heard Cara got the okay for the auction and that she was going to look for something else in the old broken storage room, you panicked. You followed her and waited for the perfect opportunity, then pushed her inside and locked the trunk. You figured you could grab the art when the ship hit port and then disappear with no one the wiser."

"You're all crazy." Lance turned around to run.

"Freeze, Lance Bateman," Special Agent Amy Randolph said. "You're coming with me." She grabbed his arm and handcuffed him, then slipped her gun in her holster. "I'll take it from here, Captain."

"No, you won't," said two firm voices.

We all whirled around.

There stood Brie and Haden Gray, each holding a gun and a badge out in front of them.

Sunny grabbed my arm. *Well, that's a twist I didn't see coming.*

"Who are you guys?" Amy looked between the two of them and then at Captain Hughes. "Did you know about this?"

"I know everything that happens on my ship, Randolph." The captain narrowed her eyes. "These two FBI agents are special agents who've been undercover for the past year, posing as a married couple of photographers on all of our ships."

"That's right. I'm Special Agent Jessica Parker, and this is my partner, Special Agent Ethan Cole."

"We've been tracking an art smuggling ring up and down the east coast on different ships from this cruise line," Ehtan stated. "Each ship has a person planted who steals a piece of the art and then smuggles it off during one of the island stops. It's easier that way, with less security than to bring it back to a US port."

"We knew these plants weren't working alone," Jessica said. "They were usually desperate for money for one reason or another, like Lance to pay for the treatment he needs. All of these plants report to a mastermind, but so far, this person has been elusive and savvy...until now." She looked at Amy with disgust. "I just never imaged the perp would be a dirty cop of our own."

"What gave me away?" Amy didn't even try to deny it.

"You give all your plants fake last names and credentials. Beckman in this case. You called him by his real last name, Bateman."

Amy pulled her gun back out. "I have needs." She shrugged. "We don't get nearly enough for all the danger we put ourselves in and the important work that we do to keep the world safe. My counterpart was a man. He got hired after me, and they paid him way more. That was the last straw. So, I started looking out for myself. If I didn't, no one else would."

"What are you doing?" Lance sputtered. "I don't want to die."

"You should have thought of that before you committed murder," Amy spat. "I wouldn't be on this ship if you had stuck to the plan. Instead, I had to come on board to clean up your mess."

"You know you won't get away with this." Jessica kept her raised gun trained on Amy.

"I'll shoot him." Amy held her gun to Lance's head.

"Then what?" Ethan kept his gun trained on her as well. "There are four thousand people on this ship. You don't have enough bullets to stop every one of them."

Amy shoved Lance into them, then whirled around and grabbed the captain, holding her gun to the captain's back. They were both strong, powerful women around the same height. "Something tells me *this* hostage is a little more valuable to you." Amy pulled the captain toward the elevator. "I want a speedboat ready for us. I can drive it myself, and you'll get the captain back when I reach my destination."

"Don't listen to her," Captain Hughes said, her face rigid with anger.

"You'll listen to me if you want to—"

The captain jammed her elbow back into Amy's diaphragm then rammed her fist up into her face. Amy's head snapped back, and Heather whirled around and threw Amy over her shoulder and onto the floor. Her gun skidded across the floor, which Jessica was only too happy to retrieve.

"Sorry, what was that? I didn't hear you, but you're going to listen to *me*," Heather said in a low, deadly voice as she leaned over a stunned Amy who cupped her bleeding nose. "This is *my* ship, and don't you forget it." She stood back. "Agent Parker, would you do me the honor of taking out the trash?"

Jessica hoisted Amy to her feet and cuffed her. "With pleasure, Captain."

The captain looked at Sunny and me with a raised brow. "*Now* can we go home, ladies?"

I looked at Sunny, and she nodded, replying, "All clear."

"Yes, Captain," I added. "Nothing would make us happier."

The captain went back on the bridge to oversee the trip home, while Special Agents Jessica and Ethan took Amy and Lance down to the brig with Eddie and Justin. Mitch and Nik finally joined us on the Sky Deck.

"You two missed all the excitement down below," Nik said. "It's hard work being *real* detectives."

"My hero," I said, patting his chest.

"We're so happy to have you two." Sunny kissed Mitch's cheek.

"Were you two up on stage?" Mitch asked, eying our setup. "Having a little fun playing fortune teller and sidekick?" He winked.

Sunny looked at me and took my hand. "Yup, just doing our thing." *And saving the day.*

"Amen, sister," I said. Nik gave me a funny look, so I pointed. "Look, land."

Sunny's face beamed like the day I first met her as she smiled wide and said, "We're finally home."

EPILOGUE
SUNNY

Pulling into the harbor in New York City, I had a sense of déjà vu. Once again, Mitch and I stood by the railing on the Sky Deck, looking out over the harbor. What an adventure this trip had turned out to be.

Maria and Roger stood together by the rail, deep in conversation. He had asked her to stay on board and keep traveling with him. She had agreed to start living again. It's what her Dante would have wanted.

Ivan had his arm around Natalia as they stood further down the deck, pointing at the dock, then they headed off to restock the spa. Angela and Elton stood together like a royal couple, waving to the crowd below, basking in being famous and not having to do anything until their next show. Dallas and Simon played sendoff music by the pool while they organized new games and excursions for the next cruise. Courtney and the other bartenders were already restocking the bar for the next group of people as well.

Gracie had decided she had a love of art like her father and was going to take his place in overseeing Abigail's career with Cara's help. Diana and the captain looked like they had reconciled as they stood beside the rest of the crew, ready to see the passengers off.

Meanwhile, Eddie and Justin were handling Frankie's transfer off the ship to jail, and the Dubois to the cruise ship meeting to finalize their deal, while special agents Jessica and Ethan were in charge of escorting Amy and Lance to prison where they belonged.

"I'm sorry this trip didn't turn out like you expected, Tink." Mitch slipped his big, strong arm around me and squeezed.

"Honestly, it turned out better, and you weren't even that grumpy." I winked, standing on my toes and kissing his cheek.

"We got to do some pretty cool things," Nik said from beside us. "Right Ballas?" He tweaked her nose.

She swatted his hand away. "And we made some pretty special friends I'll cherish for a lifetime. Next time, preferably on dry land."

"Sounds good to me." I looked at the dock and sucked in a breath as tears filled my eyes. "Look, Granny Gert is here with the captain."

"There's your parents." Mitch cleared his throat and slipped on a pair of sunglasses, but I saw the moisture in his eyes. "I can't wait to see our babies."

"Me, too," I said. "They are all the adventure I need."

"Oh, my Zeus," Kalli said. "Looks like our adventure has just begun."

～

Kalli

We all studied the dock just beyond my family and saw swarms of men, women, and children, waving and shouting as they ran about animatedly.

"Are those all...yours?" Sunny stared in awe, and I swear I saw Mitch force a swallow.

"Collectively, yes," I replied with a smile of pride. "They drive us crazy, but they mean well." And I couldn't wait to give them all the biggest hugs I could muster. And then sanitize in the shower, of course.

"Riiight." Mitch nodded, confirming his overwhelm at their size.

Sunny gave his arm a playful shove. "Family is family, no matter what." She smiled back at me in true understanding.

"How did Ophelia and Tasoula talk Ma into *that*?" Nik rubbed the back of his neck, his eyebrows disappearing beneath his thick head of hair.

I shielded my eyes to see better and gaped at the sight before me. "Someone's going to get hurt."

"Or arrested." Nik snorted.

Ma, Aunt Tasoula, and Chloe were all standing in full body, skin-tight wetsuits with goggles, flippers, and life jackets at the edge of the dock. If that wasn't enough of a sight, they all held hands and shouted, "Opa!" as they jumped into the ocean, clearly having consumed too much Ouzo...

Whistles blew, people shouted, and the Greek mamas splashed about yelling Marco Polo.

By the time the boat docked and we stepped off, the trio was wrapped in towels crying tears of happiness when our feet touched the ground. The four of us were surrounded as we made our way through thousands of others, reuniting with their families and friends.

"Enjoy your babies and send me pictures," I called toward Sunny as we started to separate. "You have my number, right?"

"Yes, but wait!" She grabbed Mitch and headed in our direction. "I think after all we've been through, we need a formal goodbye." Without warning, Sunny wrapped her arms around me and squeezed tight. *And don't be afraid of change. Everything is going to work out. Your future is going to be amazing and full of so much love. I predict we will see each again, my friend.* She pulled back and winked.

And I didn't feel the urge to clean my hands even once. "Thank you. I'm so glad we met."

"It was great working with you, Stevens." Mitch shook Nik's hand.

"You, too, Stone." Nik gave him a clap on the shoulder. "Give me a call if you ever need to spitball theories."

"Same here." Mitch drew his eyebrows together, his chiseled face serious once more. "C'mon, Tink, your father has Tina on his shoulders." I didn't have to read minds to know *Daddy* was home.

With one more round of quick hugs, we parted ways.

"Mystical Mavens for life!" Sunny called as she walked away.

"Mystical Mavens forever!" I echoed back and reached for Nik's hand. "You sure you want to move in with me, Detective?" I asked him right before we would enter into the fray of all our Greek blessings.

"I've never wanted anything more in my life, Ballas." He took me in his arms and leaned down with a kiss which rocked my world and soothed my soul. I felt the blush flood my face all the way to the roots of my golden blond hair...but I didn't pull away.

I didn't need to be psychic to know my future was bright, indeed.

BOOKS BY KARI LEE TOWNSEND

KALLI BALLAS MYSTERY

Mind Over Murder

Two Cents of Doom

A Touch of Malice

An Inkling of Evil

Mayhem on the Mind

Trouble for Your Thoughts

CECE MONROE MYSTERY

Harmful Habits

SUNNY MEADOWS MYSTERY

Tempest in the Tea Leaves

Corpse in the Crystal Ball

Trouble in the Tarot

Shenanigans in the Shadows

Perish in the Palm

Hazard in the Horoscope

Chaos and Cold Feet

Murder in the Meditation

SUNNY MEADOWS & KALLIE BALLAS CROSSOVER

Cruising into Danger

Road Trip to Ruin

Bachelors, Badeges & Bad Luck

DIGITAL DIVA

Talk to the Hand
Rise of the Phenoteens

BOOKS BY KARI LEE HARMON

COLDWATER COVE
Dark Seas

Frozen Waters

Dangerous Thaw

Deadly Frost

STANDALONE NOVELS
Valley of Secrets

Until Tomorrow

Project Produce

Love Lessons

LAKEHOUSE TREASURES NOVELLAS
James

Amber

Meghan

Brook

MERRY SCROOG-MAS NOVELLAS
Naughty or Nice

Sleigh Bells Ring

Jingle all the Way

TRIPLE R RANCH SHORT STORIES
Destiny Wears Spurs

Spurred by Fate

PORTRAIT OF A WOMAN

Resilient

Resourceful

Rebellious

Reclusive

ABOUT THE AUTHOR

Kari Lee Townsend is a National Bestselling Author of mysteries & a tween superhero series. She also writes romance and women's fiction as Kari Lee Harmon. With a background in English education, she's now a full-time writer, wife to her own superhero, mom of 3 sons, 1 darling diva, 1 daughter-in-law & 3 lovable fur babies. These days you'll find her walking her dogs or hard at work on her next story, living a blessed life.

www.ingramcontent.com/pod-product-compliance
Lightning Source LLC
Chambersburg PA
CBHW010542100726
47903CB00011B/3099